The Castle Of Inside Out

David Henry Wilson

Illustrations by Chris Riddell

ALMA BOOKS

ALMA BOOKS LTD
3 Castle Yard
Richmond
Surrey TW10 6TF
United Kingdom
www.almabooks.com

The Castle of Inside Out first published in 1997
This edition first published by Alma Books Limited in 2016

Text © David Henry Wilson, 1997, 2016
Illustrations and cover image © Chris Riddell, 1997, 2016

Cover design © Leo Nickolls Design

Printed in Great Britain by CPI Group (UK) Ltd, Croydon CR0 4YY

ISBN: 978-1-84688-396-5

For Lisbeth, with love

Chapter One

THE BLACK RABBIT

"You should know," said the black rabbit, "that there are two kinds of people at the Castle. The insiders live inside – they're lovely. They're well behaved and kind and properly educated and civilized. Insiders are good. And then there are the outsiders. They live outside. They're horrible. Ugh! Outsiders are disgusting – loud and crude, rough and rude. And green. Do you know what those green people would do to me if they caught me? Do you?"

"No," said Lorina.

"They'd eat me. That's what they'd do."

"How awful!" said Lorina.

"You can say that again," said the black rabbit.

"How awful!" said Lorina again.

"And that," said the black rabbit, "is why I never set foot outside the forest. I'll show you the way, but don't expect me to take you there."

He stomped through the fallen leaves, and Lorina followed a few paces behind, thinking about the green people. It would be nice to see the Castle and the insiders, but not so nice to bump into the outsiders.

"If the green people would eat you," said Lorina, "maybe they'd eat me as well."

"I wouldn't be surprised," said the black rabbit. "They'll eat anything. And anybody."

"Have you *never* left the forest?" asked Lorina.

"Never," said the black rabbit. "Forest born and forest bred. I'll only leave here when I'm dead."

"But if you've never left the forest," said Lorina, "how do you know about the insiders and the outsiders?"

"Everyone knows about them," said the black rabbit. "It's what's called 'common knowledge'."

"*I* don't know about them," said Lorina.

"Then you're ignorant," said the black rabbit.

"I don't think I'm ignorant," said Lorina.

"That's the worst type of ignorance," said the black rabbit. "When people don't know they're ignorant."

It was quite difficult to talk to the black rabbit – not only because all Lorina could see was his black bottom bobbing up and down, but also because he seemed to know so much. When Lorina had met him in the forest, he'd known straight away who she was and where she was going and why she was going there.

"School project, eh, Lorina?" he'd said. "And you're looking for the Castle."

Lorina had to write about "A Special Place", and the Castle had come into her mind the moment Mr Blair had set the subject. Her sister had talked about it once, when she'd been reading a strange book. Edith was always reading strange books. Lorina had asked her where the Castle was, but all Edith said was: "Oh, somewhere on the other side of the forest." And she'd never mentioned insiders or outsiders – or black rabbits, for that matter.

The forest was getting thinner now, and Lorina noticed a lot of stumps, although there was no sign of fallen trees.

"That's the green people's doing," said the black rabbit. "Vandals. They cut 'em down and take 'em away. Soon there'll be no forest left, and then where will I live?"

"How do you know it's them?" asked Lorina.

"Everybody knows it's the green people," said the black rabbit.

"Have you actually seen them?" persisted Lorina, who didn't like losing arguments.

"Of course I haven't seen 'em," snapped the black rabbit. "If I'd seen them, they'd have seen me, and I'd have ended up as a pie."

"But if you haven't seen them," said Lorina, "you can't even be sure they exist."

The black rabbit stopped, turned, looked up at Lorina and shook his head in disbelief.

"I sometimes think," he sniffed, "that ignorance is a disease. Have you ever seen Australia?"

"No," said Lorina.

"Have you seen the Battle of Hastings, the inside of a cow's stomach, the other side of the moon or a dinosaur's poo?"

"No."

"Then how do you know *they* exist? Or existed?"

Lorina thought for a moment. This needed working out.

"Well, I've heard about them," she said.

"And now you've heard about the green people," said the black rabbit, and marched on.

They had reached the edge of the forest. There were scarcely any trees, and the carpet of leaves had become threadbare, while the air itself smelt faintly of burning. Ahead of them was a steep slope.

"This is as far as I go," said the black rabbit. "You see that hill?"

"Yes," said Lorina.

"Of course, it's only there because you see it," scoffed the black rabbit. "And if you couldn't see it, you'd say it wasn't there… Well, go to the top of it, and you'll see the Castle. The insiders are inside, but watch out for the outsiders. They're outside. Good luck. One word of advice: never argue with someone who knows more than you do. You can't win."

With that, he was off, bounding through the dead undergrowth as if he'd seen a pastry dish with long ears.

Chapter Two

THE GREEN PEOPLE

From the top of the hill, Lorina could see the Castle. It too stood on a hill, on the other side of a bare, brown valley that was only just visible through a haze of smoke. The smoke itself seemed to be coming down from the Castle, which was surprising because, although it was autumn, the day was quite warm – certainly not cold enough for a fire. Lorina wondered if the insiders had thin skin.

She set off down the hill and across the smoky valley, keeping a sharp lookout for the green outsiders as she walked. She didn't believe the black rabbit, but on the other hand, she didn't disbelieve him either, which gave her a funny feeling of wanting to go on and wanting to turn back. She remembered once hearing about people who ate people. They were called cannonballs.

The closer Lorina came to Castle Hill, the thicker grew the air, and soon she found herself coughing. Suddenly, she became aware of some brown cone shapes jutting out of the brown soil. There were lots of them, and at first she thought they might be sheaves of corn, but then, to her surprise, two tiny figures emerged from one and came running towards her. They were green.

Lorina stopped. The black rabbit had been right, then, and maybe it *was* time to turn back.

"Hello!" cried one of the figures, still some distance away, and the voice was that of a child. "Hello! Hello!"

Soon they were close enough for Lorina to see just how tiny they were – only about as tall as her leg. Their green bodies were quite naked, and they were very thin, running on matchstick legs balanced above by matchstick arms. One was a girl and one was a boy, and the latter was shy and stayed a few paces behind the girl.

"Have you brought us something to eat?" asked the girl, looking up at Lorina with eyes that seemed much too big for her face.

"No," said Lorina. "No, I haven't."

Two little faces fell.

"I'm sorry," said Lorina. "Should I have done?"

The girl didn't answer, but instead ran her hand over Lorina's dress. The black rabbit had been wrong after all. These little green people would have stroked him, not eaten him.

The girl took Lorina's hand, and then Lorina took the hand of the boy, and they walked together towards the sheaves, which were actually tents.

"My name's Tanga. What's yours?" asked the girl.

"Lorina," said Lorina.

"That's a funny name," said Tanga. "My brother's Birim."

At the sound of the voices, more green children emerged from the tents, and then green adults came too, though none of them were taller than Lorina's shoulder. They were all thin, and most of them walked in slow motion, as if their matchstick arms and legs were too heavy to move.

The children all wanted to touch Lorina's dress, and kept asking for food, while the adults hung back. Tanga would not let Lorina stop, and so the crowd accompanied them all the way to the entrance of Tanga's tent. Only when Tanga pulled Lorina inside did the slow movement cease, and the adults and children crouched down on the dry brown earth to wait.

Inside Tanga's tent lay a woman. She coughed, then moved her head and looked at Lorina through half-open eyes.

"Hello," said Lorina.

The woman nodded, and coughed again.

"This is Lorina," said Tanga. "This is my mother. She's very ill. Can you help her?"

"Oh dear," said Lorina, and sat down beside the sick woman. "What's the matter with you?"

The woman shook her head.

"There's nothing the matter with her," said Tanga. "She's just ill."

"But is it measles, mumps, chickenpox, whooping cough?" asked Lorina.

"She's dying," said Birim. They were the first words he'd spoken, and they made Lorina shiver. Dying, she knew, was the worst of all illnesses.

"We're all dying," said a deep voice, and Lorina turned to see a green man standing in the entrance.

"If we don't starve, the smoke will kill us. We thought perhaps you'd come to help us."

"Well, no," said Lorina. "I'm doing a project for Mr Blair."

"Is he in the Castle?" asked the man.

"No, he's my teacher," answered Lorina. "But I'm on my way to the Castle. Perhaps someone there can help you."

The green man smiled, and Lorina saw that he had very white, even teeth.

"They can," he said. "But they won't."

He left the tent, and Lorina heard him say something to the people outside. There was a loud sigh.

"I'm ever so sorry," said Lorina. "I would help if I could."

The woman had closed her eyes. Lorina put her hand on the woman's forehead, which was what people usually did when someone was ill, and she found it icy cold.

"Oh dear," said Lorina. "Maybe she could have a bowl of soup to warm her up."

But little Tanga said there was no soup. There was no food of any kind.

"Do they have food in the Castle, then?" asked Lorina.

"Of course they do," said Tanga.

"Then I'll go and get some," said Lorina.

She stepped out of the tent. The crowd had dispersed, and only the man with white teeth was standing outside.

"I'm going to the Castle," said Lorina, "to get some food."

The man nodded.

"You have a kind heart," he said. "Tell me – are you young or old?"

"Oh, I'm very young," said Lorina, surprised.

"Ah," said the man, "perhaps that's why."

"Are you Tanga's father?" asked Lorina.

"No," said the man. "Her father is dead. I'm Qasim. I am father to all these people, and can help none."

"Why do you all stay here in this smoke?" asked Lorina.

"Because there is nowhere else for us to go," answered Qasim. "The Castle is our home, and elsewhere is the home of others."

Lorina would have liked to talk longer with Qasim. Although he was so small, the depth of his voice and the dignity of his bearing made him seem tall. He could be father to all people. She wanted to ask him why there was no food, and why the insiders would not send help, and what they were like, but there was no time for questions. Tanga and Birim's mother needed help now.

And so Lorina hurried away to the foot of the hill, and then began her climb upwards through the thickening smoke towards the Castle.

Chapter Three

INSIDE THE CASTLE

The gate to the Castle was huge. It was higher than a house, and was built of thick oak, and as she stood before it, Lorina wished she *had* asked Qasim what the insiders were like. If they needed a gate this high, they must be giants, and Lorina now began to wonder if the black rabbit had got things the wrong way round. The green people were well behaved and kind, so maybe the insiders were the rough cannonballs.

Surprisingly, there was a doorbell that was waist-high to Lorina, and although she was a little frightened, she bent down and pressed it. After a moment's pause, there was a woody scrape, and then a squeaky voice said: "Who are yer?"

"Lorina," said Lorina.

"Whaddyerwant?" asked the squeak.

"To come in," said Lorina.

"Oh!" said the squeak.

There was another scrapy noise, this time more metallic, and it was followed by a creak as a little door right in front of Lorina swung open.

"Come on then," squeaked the voice, and Lorina found herself looking down at a bright-eyed little creature with whiskers and a very twitchy nose. He was a doormouse.

Lorina stooped, because the door only came up to the level of her chest, and stepped through.

"If you're so small," she said to the doormouse, "why do you have such a big gate?"

"If you're so nosy," said the doormouse, "why d'yer 'ave such a tiny nose? Now then, who are yer, an' whaddyerwant?"

"I told you who I am," said Lorina. "I'm Lorina."

"Just checkin'," said the doormouse. "An' yer wanner come in, right?"

"Yes," said Lorina.

"Why?" asked the doormouse.

"Because I want to get help for the green people," answered Lorina.

"Hmmm!" hmmmed the doormouse. "Not much of a reason. Well, foller me."

Lorina followed him through the mighty archway that housed the gate, and found herself facing a large courtyard enclosed by buildings that towered high into the sky. She noticed that the air was free of smoke.

"Come on, come on," said the doormouse, and Lorina followed him through a low door into a stuffy little room with a chair, a desk and a tall, long-legged bird who was sitting on the other side of the desk. She had a number of pens stuck in her crest, and was using one of these to paint the toenails of her left foot. She was a secretary bird.

"Name's Lorina," said the doormouse. "Says she wants to 'elp the green people."

"Sit down," said the secretary bird.

Lorina sat down, and the doormouse left the room. There followed a long silence, during which the secretary bird finished the toenails of her left foot and turned her attention to those of her right foot.

"Is anything going to happen?" asked Lorina.

"Won't be long now," said the secretary bird.

"I'm in a bit of a hurry," said Lorina.

"We're doing all we can," said the secretary bird.

There followed another long silence, during which the secretary bird finished the toenails of her right foot, and started touching up the toenails of her left foot.

"Excuse me," said Lorina, "but there are people starving outside, and—"

"We won't keep you long," said the secretary bird, "but we are rather busy."

Lorina was about to say that painting toenails wasn't her idea of being busy, when a door in the wall behind the secretary bird was suddenly thrust open. In came a sharp-featured, whiskered animal with shifty eyes that looked past rather than at Lorina. He was a bureaurat.

"I'll see you now," he said.

Lorina stood up and followed him into the second office.

"Is the whole castle run by animals?" she asked.

"I'll ask the questions," said the bureaurat, and motioned to Lorina to be seated.

The second office was a lot bigger than the first, and every wall was covered with shelves full of files. The only gap was in the wall behind the bureaurat's desk, and this was taken up with a large picture of a smiling pig. Underneath was a label that said "OUR BELOVED LEADER". The rat sat down, opened a file on his desk, picked up a pen and wrote something.

"Now then," he said, without looking up. "Name?"

"Lorina," said Lorina.

"Date of death?"

"Don't you mean date of birth?" asked Lorina.

"I know what I mean," said the rat. "Date of death?"

"I don't know," said Lorina.

"Don't know," wrote the rat. "Length of left leg from knee to ankle?"

"I don't know," said Lorina.

"Don't know," wrote the rat. "Number of hairs on your head?"

"I don't know," said Lorina.

"Hm," sniffed the rat. "You don't know much about yourself, do you?"

"I can't be expected to know *that* sort of thing," replied Lorina.

"Well, if *you* don't know it," rasped the rat, "who will? Favourite colour?"

"Green," said Lorina.

"Red," said the rat.

"No, it's green!" said Lorina.

"Red is *my* favourite colour," said the rat.

"Oh, I thought you were asking me for mine," said Lorina.

"No point in asking you about yourself," said the rat, "because you don't know anything."

"I don't see the point of *any* of these questions," said Lorina. "All I want is some help for the green people."

"You can't get help till I've filled in these forms," said the rat.

"Then let's fill them in and be done with them," said Lorina.

"Favourite food?" asked the rat.

"Chocolate," said Lorina.

"Bad for your teeth," said the rat. "I'll put cheese."

"This is ridiculous," said Lorina. "If you're not going to help me, then let me see someone who will."

"You can't see anyone," said the rat, "until I've given you a permit."

"A permit for what?" asked Lorina.

"A permit to enter the Castle," replied the rat.

"But I've already entered the Castle," said Lorina.

"No you haven't," said the rat, "because no one can enter the Castle without a permit. Now sign here."

He pushed a piece of paper and a pen across to Lorina, and she wrote her signature at the bottom of the sheet. Then the bureaurat took it from her, stamped it with a stamp, stamped it with another stamp, stamped it again, restamped it, overstamped it, understamped it, put it on the floor, where he stamped, stumped and stomped on it, picked it up and handed it to Lorina.

"Your permit," he said.

"Thank you," said Lorina. "Now where would you advise me to go?"

"Home," said the rat.

"I mean, to get help for the green people," said Lorina.

"Anywhere at all," said the rat. "It won't make the slightest difference."

Lorina asked him who was in charge of the Castle's food, and was told that it was a Mr Hogg, who would probably be in the Castle kitchen.

"And where's the kitchen?" asked Lorina.

"You ask too many questions," snapped the rat. Lorina stood up to go.

"One moment," said the rat. "Let me see your permit." Lorina handed it to him, and he studied it carefully.

"All right, everything's in order," he said. "Off you go."

"Aren't you going to give me my permit back?" asked Lorina.

"Certainly not," said the rat. "All permits have to be filed in my office."

"Then what was the point in giving it to me?" asked Lorina.

"If I hadn't given it to you," said the bureaurat, "you couldn't have shown it to me, could you?"

Chapter Four

MR HOGG

"Fat, fat, let me be fat,
Or let me be even fatter than that.
Let me be beefy, bulky, obese,
Give me some food, and let me increase.

Let me be corpulent, let me be stout,
Inflating the tubes is what life's all about.
Empty the saucepan, pile up the plate,
Pour on the gravy, pump up the weight.

Let the flesh wobble like joggles of jelly,
Give me a bulging balloon for a belly.
Open the jaws, lift up the hand,
Lie back and watch the elastic expand.

Grub, grub, fetch me more grub,
A plate is too small, so bring me a tub.

For never, no never can I have enough
Of this stomach-extendingly stupendous stuff."

The sound of Mr Hogg's voice reached Lorina's ears long before the sight of his body reached her eyes. But in spite of the words of his song, she was certainly not prepared for what she saw when she entered the kitchen. Sitting at the table was a quivering mountain of rubbery blubbery pink. It was a gigantic blob of shapeless flesh that wobbled in huge folds all the way down to the floor, on which Lorina could just make out the shattered remains of a chair. And at the top of this heaving, sagging mass was a face that consisted entirely of a cavernously gaping mouth. Lorina had never seen any animal like this before. It was a monster.

On the kitchen table in front of the monster was a pile of food that grew ever taller and wider, as someone from behind ladled dollop onto dollop over dollop.

"If you were a balloon," said Lorina, "you'd burst."

"And if you were a polite little girl," said the monster, "you'd say 'Excuse me' and 'May I come in?'"

"Excuse me, and may I come in?" asked Lorina.

"You are in," said the monster. "You should now say 'Excuse me' and 'May I go out?'"

"Well, excuse me," said Lorina, "and may I talk to you?"

"No," said the monster. "I have to get on with my work."

"Work?" cried Lorina.

"Work," said the monster. "Come on, come on, fetch me more grub!" He was now talking to the unseen creature behind the food mountain, and the speed of the dolloping doubled.

Now the monster began to scoop great portions of "work" into his chomping jaws, and Lorina watched in amazement as a shepherd's pie, a cottage pie and a pumpkin pie rose into the air and disappeared.

"Well," he said, "whajewa?"

"I beg your pardon?" asked Lorina.

"Whajewa?" asked the monster through a brimming caveful of steak and onions, peas and cabbage, roast potatoes and Yorkshire pudding.

"I want some food for the green people," said Lorina.

"Casparit," said the monster through hamburger, chips and tomato ketchup.

"What?" asked Lorina.

"Ca-spar-it!" repeated the monster.

"Of course you can spare it," said Lorina. "That plateful alone is enough to feed fifty."

"Goway!"

"I won't go away!"

The monster swallowed a collection of chicken breasts, leeks, runner beans and artichokes, and for just a moment stopped scooping.

"In that case," he said, "sit still and keep quiet till I've finished. You're ruining my concentration."

"But people are starving out there!" said Lorina.

"And people will be starving in here if I don't get on with my work!" snapped the monster, grabbing a shoal of fried fish with baked beans and tartare sauce.

Lorina sat still, kept quiet and watched the monster gobbling. Suddenly, she realized that something was happening to his face. As the mighty jaws moved round and round and up and down and from side to side, a little pair of eyes peeped out from the top of the face, and two snouty black holes appeared in front of them.

"Now I know what you're doing," said Lorina. "You're making a pig of yourself."

"That's why he's cookalled Mr Hogg," said a high voice from under the table.

Lorina looked down, and saw a blue-faced bird with dark-grey wings, a light-grey chest and a white cap on its head. It was a cookoo.

"No use cookoming to him for help," whispered the cookoo.

"Where shall I go, then?" asked Lorina.

"The fields," whispered the cookoo.

"Grub!" yelled the monster, and the cookoo disappeared for a moment to ladle some pizza, quiche, lentils, asparagus, sausages and scrambled egg onto the pile. Then he was back again.

"How will I get to the fields?" asked Lorina.

"Take a horse and cookat," whispered the cookoo.

"Cookat?" asked Lorina.

"The cookat drives the cookart," whispered the cookoo. "You'll find them in the cookart park."

"Thank you," said Lorina.

"Cookood luck!" said the cookoo.

And so, as Mr Hogg downed a mouthful of pheasant, new potatoes, broccoli and green apples, Lorina left the kitchen and went in search of the cookart park.

Chapter Five

IN THE FIELDS

There were surprisingly few animals wandering round the Castle, and most of those that Lorina did see were dogs. One of them asked her where she was going and then gave her directions (he was a guide dog). She noticed that the picture of the smiling pig – "OUR BELOVED LEADER" – was stuck on many of the walls, and there were even some statues of him in the different courtyards. She wondered if perhaps Mr Hogg was the leader, and had eaten himself shapeless.

The cart park was on the south side of the Castle, and it was from here that Lorina had to take a horse and cat out into the fields. It was only when she approached the cat and told him where she wanted to go that she realized she had a problem.

"Two piaounds," said the cat, who had a black coat and green eyes.

"Oh," said Lorina. "I haven't got any money."

"Niao money," said the cat, "niao journey."

"But I must go to the fields," said Lorina, "to get some food for the green people. Won't you take me for nothing, just this once?"

"Niaobody does things for niaothing," said the cat. "What's that riaound your hair?

"A ribbon," said Lorina.

"That'll do," said the cat, and so Lorina gave him the ribbon and climbed up onto the cart.

As they drove out of the Castle, the cat told Lorina that the fields were to the siaouth, and his cart was often used to transport food. He also went to the niaorth, where the forests were, in order to bring back tree trunks. He'd seen the green people outside, and the woodcutters sometimes gave them food.

"But you won't get food for them niaow," he said.

"Why not?" asked Lorina.

"You'll see," said the cat.

They drove down the hill, and already Lorina could see the fields. They were quite different from the burnt brown land on the northern side. These were green and rich, and were covered with plants of various shapes, hues and sizes. Soon she could see figures digging, sowing, reaping and gathering, and to her surprise she realized that they were green people. They were singing, but although their song was a happy one, their voices sounded strangely flat and tired:

"Isn't it wonderful,
Isn't it grand,
For me and my wife
To be spending our life
Working the land?

Oh what an honour,
Once you begin,
With your seeds in a sack
Bending your back
To put 'em all in.

Oh what a pleasure
After the seeding
To watch the plants grow
With your hands full of hoe,
Happily weeding.

Oh what a joy
To be running all day
Without any rest,
Chasing each pest
Far, far away.

Let us work on,
Let nothing intrude,
For we'd rather die
Than fail to supply
Our Castle with food.

When crops are ready
We're filled with delight,
Picking and fetching,
Bending and stretching
From daybreak till night."

Lorina noticed that these green people were not nearly as thin as those on the north side of the Castle, and they were able to move much faster. There were some dogs among them, but they weren't working. She also saw a crackling fire over in a distant corner, and some of the green people were carrying loads of plants towards it.

"That's strange," said Lorina. "I wonder what they're doing."

"Ask the boss," said the cat. "He'll tell you what it's all abiaout."

They drove towards the fire, and now Lorina could see that the green people were carrying all sorts of vegetables – potatoes, carrots, beans, cabbages, onions, tomatoes – and to her horror, she realized that they were being thrown on the fire.

"Stop! Stop!" she cried, jumping off the cart, and running towards the blaze. "Don't burn them! Stop! Stop!"

The green people did stop, and all turned to look at the intruder.

"Who's the boss?" asked Lorina.

"Oi am," said a voice from beyond the flames, "an' what d'you think you'm a-doin'? Keep that foire a-blazin'!"

Lorina rushed round to the other side, and found a strange creature that was wearing a thick brownish overcoat, which made its body seem far too big for its legs. Its face was horny-skinned, and poking out from the coat were two large, very sharp claws. It was a farmadillo.

"Please don't burn the vegetables!" cried Lorina. "We can use them to feed…"

She was going to say "the green people", but there were green people all around her.

"…To feed the hungry," she said.

"Can't use these ter feed nobody," said the farmadillo. "These are for burnin'. Keep 'em comin' there, you lazy lot!"

The green people were throwing their loads on the fire again.

"No, no, you don't understand!" said Lorina. "On the other side of the Castle there are green people who are starving. We can use all this food to feed them."

"You'm the one who don't unnerstand," said the farmadillo. "This food ain't fer feedin'. This food's fer burnin'."

"But it's good food!" cried Lorina.

"Course it's good food," said the farmadillo. "'Tis the best. Oi only produces the best."

"Why does it have to be burnt?" asked Lorina.

"We'm exceedin' our quota," said the farmadillo.

"What's a quota?" asked Lorina.

"A quota," said the farmadillo, "is the thing wot we'm exceedin'. Now you'd best get out the way afore oi 'as you mistaken fer a turnip."

"But don't you care about the green people on the other side?" cried Lorina.

"Do yer think they cares about me an' my quota?" asked the farmadillo.

"No," said Lorina.

"So whoi should oi care about them?" said the farmadillo. "Keep the foire a-blazin'! Now go away afore oi sets the dogs on yer."

Lorina found his attitude very annoying. All this good food was being wasted, and yet there was nothing she could do. Already three black dogs were heading towards her, and so she hurried back to the horse and cat. But just as she was about to climb up, a little green woman plucked at her dress.

"If you want to know about quotas," she whispered, "go to the piggy bank."

Lorina wanted to ask her some questions, but she scurried away – obviously afraid that the farmadillo or the dogs would see her.

Lorina climbed up beside the cat.

"Hiaow did you get on?" he asked.

"Not very well," said Lorina.

"Didn't think you would," said the cat.

Lorina asked him if he knew what quotas were, but he didn't, and so she said she wanted to go to the piggy bank.

"Two piaounds," said the cat.

"Oh dear," said Lorina.

"What's that riaound your neck?" asked the cat.

"Beads," said Lorina.

"They'll do," said the cat.

On the way, Lorina asked him about the Beloved Leader.

"He's a pig," said the cat.

"Yes, I know," said Lorina. "Is he the pig that runs the piggy bank?"

"Niao," said the cat, "that's another pig."

"Then is he Mr Hogg, who's in charge of the food?"

"Niao, that's another pig as well."

"Are the pigs in charge of everything, then?" asked Lorina.

"Of course they are," said the cat.

"Why?" asked Lorina.

"Because only pigs want to be in charge," said the cat.

He drove her back up the hill, and through the southern gate to a building with iron bars over the windows and a gold sign that read: "PIGGY BANK. LEAVE ALL YOUR MONEY HERE".

"He won't be very pleased to see you," said the cat.

"Why not?" asked Lorina, climbing down from the cart.

"Because you haven't got any money to leave him. Ciaow!"

Chapter Six

THE
PIGGY BANKER

The piggy banker was sitting in his bath, washing himself with gold coins. As he ran them tinklingly over his fat pink body, he sang this song:

"You gotta have money
If you wanna be rich.
If you ain't got money,
You'll end up in a ditch.
So you won't find me
Steeped in povertee,
Rich, rich, rich is what I'm gonna be.

Taxes here,
Taxes there,
I'll put taxes
On everything you wear,

Everything you read,
Everything you feed,
Everything you earn and everything you need.

Tear your hair,
Say it isn't fair,
I don't care
Cos I'm a billionaire.
You can peak and pine,
I feel fine,
So long as all your money ends up as being mine."

"I don't think that's very nice," said Lorina.

"It is for me," said the piggy banker. "And I'm the one that matters. Pass me that thousand-pound note, will you? I want to blow my nose."

"Why don't you use a handkerchief, like everybody else?" asked Lorina.

"Because I'm not like everybody else," said the pig. "I'm the piggy banker. Now then, how much are you going to give me?"

"Nothing," said Lorina. "I want to know what quotas are."

"Why?" asked the pig.

"The farmadillo says he can't give food to the green people in the north because of quotas," said Lorina. "What are they?"

"A quota," said the pig rather grandly, "is what you are allowed. And you aren't allowed to give food to the green people."

"Why not?" asked Lorina.

"It's all very complicated," said the pig, rather less grandly. "It's a matter of echonomics, and you wouldn't understand."

"What are echonomics?" asked Lorina.

"Exactly!" said the pig. "I told you you wouldn't understand."

"Then explain it to me," said Lorina.

"Well," said the pig, "if you gave free food to the green people, *everybody* would want free food. That's the 'echo'. I'm not sure about the 'nomics'."

"Then why don't you give money to the green people," suggested Lorina, "so that they can buy the food?"

"You can't give money away!" said the pig. "Don't be stupid! Money isn't to be given away. Money is to be kept. Here. By me."

"But the green people are starving!" cried Lorina. "And the farmadillo is burning food! It doesn't make sense!"

"Of course it makes sense," said the pig. "It's the perfect system."

"It's a silly system!" cried Lorina. "It's cruel and it's selfish, and so are you! Why won't you help the green people?"

"Help them? Help them? Because, my dear little girl," said the pig, "it's none of my business. Whether they starve or don't starve is their concern, not mine. My concern is money. The cashiest, coiniest, notiest concern in the world. Now pass me my bathrabbit, will you?"

He pointed towards the door, and there, hanging on a hook, was a large white rabbit. Lorina reached up and, as she lifted the bathrabbit down, it whispered in her ear:

"Go and see the PandA."

"Who's the PandA?" Lorina whispered back.

"Philanthropy and Aid," whispered the rabbit.

"Thank you," whispered Lorina.

She would have liked to ask what "Philanthropy" was, but the piggy banker had already grabbed the bathrabbit and was draping it round his shoulders as he climbed out of the coin-filled bath.

"Take my advice," he said. "Forget the green people. Happiness is money, and money is happiness. That's all we know on earth, and all we need to know."

Chapter Seven

THE PANDA

The PandA lived in a tiny building, on the door of which was a notice that filled Lorina with hope. It read:

We're here to help the needy,
We're here to help the sick.
If you want aid
Don't be afraid,
Cos we can do the trick.

Lorina knocked at the door. There was no answer. She knocked again, and when again there was no answer, she opened the door and stepped inside. She found herself in a shop full of empty shelves.

"Hello!" she called. "Anybody there?"

"Oh! Ooooh! Aaaaah!" said a sleepy voice.

It came from one corner of the store, and lying there was a large animal with a white face, black ears and black eyes, one of which was open and one of which was shut.

"Can I help you?" he asked.

"I hope so," said Lorina, and told him all about the starving green people in the north, and the pigs who had refused to help, and the need to get food to her friends as soon as possible.

"Ts, ts," said the PandA, "that's terrible, that's really terrible. Just hold on a moment."

Without getting up, he reached out for a little notebook and flicked through the pages.

"Green people… green people… north… north… Yes, we sent them some bread last Tuesday with the timber wagon. I suppose they've finished that, have they?"

"Yes," said Lorina.

"Ts, ts," said the PandA, "terrible, terrible. It's always the same story. You give them bread, they finish it and then they want some more. It's never-ending."

"I have three meals a day at home," said Lorina.

"So do I," said the PandA. "It's the best way."

"But the green people are only getting one meal a week!" said Lorina.

"Terrible," said the PandA. "Ts, ts, terrible."

"So will you help them?" asked Lorina.

"No," said the PandA.

"No?" cried Lorina.

"No," said the PandA. "I would if I could, but I can't."

"Why not?" cried Lorina.

"No food," said the PandA. "And no money."

"But the notice on your door says you're here to help the needy!" cried Lorina.

"And so I am," said the PandA. "I'll help anyone and everyone, so long as it doesn't cost anything."

This was too much for Lorina. She had bravely gone from one hope to another, and every one had been dashed. Now it seemed she would never be able to help Tanga and Birim, or their mother, or Qasim, and all of them would die. She sat on the floor and put her head in her hands.

The PandA stood up, padded across to her, put a paw round her shoulder and said, "There, there."

"I just don't know what to do," said Lorina.

"There's only one thing you can do," said the PandA.

"What's that?" asked Lorina.

"The same as me," said the PandA. "Go to sleep."

But Lorina had no intention of going to sleep. Going to sleep would not help anybody, she said.

"It helps me," said the PandA.

Lorina had a good think. Even if she couldn't get food for the green people, at least she might be able to stop the smoke. She hadn't even tried to do that yet. She might need money to buy things, but surely she wouldn't need money to stop things.

"You need money for everything," said the PandA. "Except sleep. You can get as much sleep as you like for absolutely nothing."

But Lorina had made up her mind and, as the PandA padded back to his corner, she stood up, pushed her ribbonless hair back behind her ears and set off on her next quest.

Chapter Eight

HOOFBALL

Lorina didn't get very far. No sooner had she set foot outside the PandA's door than she found herself caught up in a seething mass of excited animals. They were all heading in the same direction, and she had no choice but to go along with them. Some were dressed in yellow, some in purple, and they had scarves and flags and rattles of the same colour.

"Where are we going?" she asked a donkey dressed completely in yellow.

"Hoofball!" he brayed. "We're going to win the cup, we're going to win the cup, hee-haw, hee-haw, we're going to win the cup!"

"What's hoofball?" asked Lorina.

"Hee hee, haw haw, she doesn't know what hoofball is!" shrieked the donkey.

"It's a game," said an ass in purple. "And today's the Cup Final – Donkaster Rovers against Assenal."

The crowd swept Lorina along into a large court-yard, where there were already hundreds of animals singing at the tops of their voices: "Don-keys! Don-keys!" or "As-ses! As-ses!" As well as door-mice, secretary birds, bureaurats, cookoos, horses and cats, farmadillos and bathrabbits, there were carpanthers, mechangaroos, chimpanzee-sweeps, undertigers, glass-boas, allicaterers, hippopotters, photogophers, physioterrapins, steeplejackals, moosicians, rhinoceramists, haredressers, newt-agents, osteopythons, grebegrocers and, all alone in a box, speaking non-stop into a lollipop, a commanteater.

Suddenly, all the spectators in yellow started cheering wildly, as the donkey team ran out into the playing area. "Come on, you yellows!" they chanted. "Come on, you yellows!"

Then the spectators in purple let out an equally wild cheer, as the asses took to the field. "Come on, you purples!" they brayed. "Come on, you purples!"

Next, an extraordinary creature ran onto the pitch: he had very long legs, a very long neck, was dressed in black and was blowing a whistle. He was the girafferee.

The two teams lined up, facing a balcony that overlooked the courtyard, and onto this balcony there now stepped the unmistakable, smiling figure of the Beloved Leader. He was accompanied by some other pigs, who hung back a pace or two behind him. He waved to the crowd, but they took no notice because they were still cheering for the yellows or purples.

"Wave to the Piggident!" snarled an angry voice, and Lorina found herself looking into the accusing eyes of a large black dog. He was one of several circulating among the spectators, and soon everyone was waving to the Beloved Leader, who smiled even more graciously.

Then from somewhere came the sound of music and, at the command of the dogs, everyone began to sing:

"We love our glorious leader,
We'll serve him all day long,
Our Piggident, our Piggident,
Oh he can do no wrong.
Hero so fine,

Sweetest of swine,
May he live for ever,
Our Piggident divine."

The dogs told everyone to cheer, and so they cheered, and the Beloved Leader smiled again, waved again and at last sat down.

When the game began, Lorina found it very difficult to follow. It consisted of the donkeys and the asses all running after a ball (or each other), and kicking the ball (or each other). The yellow spectators cheered when the donkeys kicked the ball (or an ass), and the purple spectators cheered when the asses kicked the ball (or a donkey). The girafferee occasionally blew his whistle, and then half the spectators booed and half of them cheered.

Lorina soon got bored, and started looking round the crowd. She was hoping to see some green people, but there were none. Perhaps they were still working in the fields. If only the northern green people could get to the south, she thought – at least they would have enough to eat. Did the southern green people live inside the Castle, she wondered, or were they outsiders too? And why was no one willing to help the northern green people?

Her thoughts were interrupted by a loud roar. The boring game had suddenly taken a dramatic turn. One of the asses had kicked the ball into a net, and all the purple spectators were cheering, while the yellow spectators were booing. Then the donkeys started kicking the asses, the asses kicked the donkeys, the yellow spectators started fighting the purple spectators, the purple spectators fought back, and in no time the whole courtyard was covered in fighting animals.

"What are they fighting for?" asked Lorina.

"Because it should never have been allowed!" screamed a yellow carpanther.

"Oh yes it should!" roared a purple undertiger, and leapt at the carpanther's throat.

Lorina had never seen such a commotion, and she was just wondering how it was all going to end when racing into the midst of the battle came a pack of snapping, snarling, biting, barking dogs. Within a few minutes, they had driven the spectators back to the sides of the courtyard, leaving a carpet of bodies out on the playing area. These were immediately carried out on stretchers by some very large, furry creatures with flasks of honey round their necks. They were stretcher-bears.

Lorina was shocked. It wasn't just the violence that shocked her – though that was bad enough. What was doubly shocking was the fact that the green people in the north were dying and nobody cared, yet when an ass kicked a ball into a net the animals cared so much that they even fought over it.

"What's the matter with all of you?" she asked a purple moosician.

"Nothing!" he boomed. "We won!"

The captain of the Assenal team now climbed some steps to the Piggident's balcony and was presented with a large gold cup, which he showed to the crowd below. The purple spectators cheered and the yellow spectators booed.

"What's in the cup?" Lorina asked a yellow haredresser.

"A million pounds, my dear, that's what's in the cup," he said.

"A million pounds!" cried Lorina. "But with a million pounds we could save all the green people!"

"With a million pounds, my dear," said the yellow haredresser, "we could buy the best ass, and then *we'd* win the cup."

Chapter Nine

THE FURNACES

After the hoofball match, Lorina asked a guide dog the way to the smoke-producing place. This turned out to be a grim, dark building with a grim, dark entrance guarded by a custoadian.

"Wharr-wharr-what do you warr-warr-want?" he asked.

As Lorina explained the problem to him, she saw two stretcher-bears carrying a body out of the building.

"Oh, what's happened?" she asked.

"That's narr-narr-nothing," croaked the custoadian. "Just anarr-narr-nother dead warr-warr-worker, that's all."

He hopped ahead of Lorina along a corridor, down a staircase, through a door, along another corridor, down another staircase and through another door into a room unlike any that Lorina had ever been in before.

It was as huge as the sky and as hot as the sun, and as she stepped inside the air wrapped itself round her like a steaming blanket. All around, dragging themselves slowly across the floor, were the drooping figures of green people fetching heavy logs, which they loaded into the furnaces in the walls. At the centre of this great cavern were wheels and pumps and engines that ground and thumped and roared as Lorina imagined prehistoric monsters must have done.

The custoadian said something to her, but it was impossible to hear his croaks above the thunderous din, and so he motioned to her to follow him. He hopped ahead of her up a narrow flight of steps, which led to a glass cabin suspended high in the roof. Lorina felt quite dizzy when she looked down. They entered the cabin, and as soon as they closed the door behind them the pounding noise was magically cut off – all but a dull rumble – and the air stopped sticking. Lorina breathed a sigh of relief.

Draped over a chair in the glass cabin was a slim, elegant creature, dressed in a reddish-brown coat with a zigzag pattern. He had a flat head with glittering eyes that studied the scene down below as he constantly swayed from side to side, backwards and forwards, round and round.

"Who is he?" Lorina whispered.

"Harr-harr-he's the superviper," replied the toad.

They waited until the superviper swung his sharp eyes towards them.

"Who'sss thisss?" he asked.

"I'm Lorina," said Lorina.

"How can I asssissst you, Lorina?"

Lorina told him that he must put the furnaces out, because the smoke was spreading over the green people and choking them.

"Nonsssenssse," hissed the superviper. "Sssoccciety needsss furnacccesss. Furnacccesss are esssential."

"But they're even killing your own workers!" said Lorina.

"We can ssspare the workersss," said the superviper, "but we can't ssspare the furnacccesss. Goodbye."

At that very moment, two of the green people down below collapsed, and were carried out.

"There you are!" said Lorina. "If you don't put out the furnaces, you'll finish up with no green people at all, either in here or out there."

"That'sss not my busssinesss," hissed the super-viper. "And it'sss not your busssinesss either, ssso go away."

The custoadian opened the door, and motioned to Lorina to accompany him.

"Shshshut that door!" hissed the snake, and once more Lorina found herself enveloped in the clinging heat and the head-bursting noise of the furnace hall.

When she reached the bottom of the narrow steps, there was a crowd of green people waiting.

"Will you help us?" they cried. "Will you save us?"

"I can't," said Lorina. "He refuses to put out the furnaces. But maybe *you* could put them out."

"If we try," said one of the green men, "he'll send in the dogs."

Suddenly, a hissing voice echoed from all sides:

"Furnacccesss ssssixxx and sssseven musssst be sssupplied at onccce. Resssume your posssstsss immediately."

The green people hurried away to feed their furnaces, but one managed to shout to her: "Go and see the Sow!" before the custoadian shooed him off.

"Who's the Sow?" asked Lorina, as soon as they were back in the cool, quiet corridor.

"Tarr-tarr-technology, Health, Environment," croaked the toad. "Sarrr-sarr-safety, Opportunity, Welfare."

"Where can I find her?" asked Lorina.

"In her starr-starr-sty, I expect," said the toad. "She likes the narr-narr-natural life. You'll smarr-smarr-smell her before you sarr-sarr-see her."

Chapter Ten

THE SOW

"Let us go back to Nature,
And be as we're meant to be.
Let cows chew the cud,
Pigs wallow in mud,
And chickens all range free.

Let each vegetable grow untainted,
A work of natural art.
Let us use manure
That's sweet and pure,
And given from bowel and heart.

Let's harness the winds and waters,
Let the air be fresh and clean.
Let our rivers flow,
Our forests grow,
And our fields be rich and green.

Let us go back to Nature,
And revel in her creations,
For in her lies the health,
From her comes the wealth
Of future generations."

"That's beautiful!" said Lorina, when the Sow had finished her song. "That's really beautiful!"

"I'm so glad you like it," said the Sow. "I just made it up. Well, I made it up some time ago actually, but I've been perfecting it. You don't think the second verse is a little… outré?"

"What's outré?" asked Lorina.

"A little… daring?"

"No, I think it's beautiful."

"Thank you so much. I really mean it. Thank you."

They were sitting in the Sow's office. Lorina had found the sty with no difficulty at all. It was on the east side of the Castle (the same side as the furnaces) and, as the custoadian had said, it reached the nose long before it reached the eyes. To Lorina's surprise, however, the Sow herself had not been in it. Some piglets were there, and mud and swill and smell, but the Sow was some distance away in a comfortable, well-furnished office with an electric light and a fridge.

"One does need to get away occasionally," she explained to Lorina, "and live in a bit of comfort. Now, what can I do for you?"

Lorina explained about the furnaces, which were killing the green people both outside and inside with their terrible smoke and fumes.

"It's got to be stopped," said Lorina, "before *all* the green people die."

"It's serious," said the Sow. "It's very serious. But is it true?"

"Of course it's true," said Lorina. "I've seen it for myself."

"Seeing isn't proving," said the Sow. "Now don't misunderstand me. I'm heartbroken, absolutely heartbroken to think of those poor green people dying. I'll do anything I can to save them. But I can't close down the furnaces just because you say it's the smoke and fumes killing them. Suppose it's something else?"

"Then go and see for yourself," said Lorina.

"And so I will," said the Sow. "As soon as I've got time."

"When will that be?" asked Lorina.

"In the near future," said the Sow.

"But the green people are dying now!" insisted Lorina.

"Heartbreaking," said the Sow. "Simply heartbreaking."

"Then do something!" cried Lorina. "They're choking and they're starving, and no one is prepared to *do* anything! You're all the same! You just don't care!"

"Now wait a minute," said the Sow. "Wait a minute. Did you say they were starving?"

"Yes," said Lorina.

"Then there's your answer," said the Sow.

"Where?" asked Lorina.

"It's not the furnaces that are killing them," said the Sow. "It's lack of food. So I'd really look a fool if I shut down the furnaces, wouldn't I? And even if the furnaces *were* killing the green people, shutting them down won't provide the green people with food – will it? – so they'll still die."

The Sow leant back, smiling, in her chair, studied one of her front trotters and started humming, "Let's get back to Nature." Lorina remembered the advice of the black rabbit: don't argue with someone who knows more than you do. But that didn't apply now, because Lorina knew more than the Sow. She mustn't lose this argument.

"In your song," she said, "you sang that the air should be fresh and clean, and the forests should grow and the fields should be rich and green."

"Yes," said the Sow.

"Do you mean it?"

"Passionately."

"Well, the air isn't fresh and clean. It's full of smoke. And the forests aren't growing – they're being cut down. And the fields aren't rich and green – they're dried up and brown. And it's all because of the furnaces."

"You're right," said the Sow, "you're absolutely right. It's one of the great problems of our time."

"Then what are you going to do about it?" persisted Lorina.

"Nothing," said the Sow.

"But you're supposed to be in charge of health and safety, and welfare, and the env… enriv…"

"Environment," said the Sow.

"So you have to do something," said Lorina, a little weakly.

"If only I could," said the Sow. "Oh, if only I could. I lie awake at nights thinking of those poor green people out... where did you say they were?"

"In the north, and in the building with the furnaces."

"Exactly. It breaks my heart, it really does. But without the furnaces, we couldn't make this lovely furniture, or enjoy the electric light, or keep our apples in the fridge. It's sad. It's tragic. It sends me into the very depths of despair. But technology comes first, as you will learn if ever you become a pig. Of course, I will fight on to the bitter end for the cause of Nature. And..."

She paused dramatically.

"And?" asked Lorina.

"Because I am so deeply moved," said the Sow, "by the dreadful suffering you have described, I'll tell you what I'm going to do."

"What?" asked Lorina.

"I'm going to set up a Commission of Inquiry," said the Sow.

"What's that?" asked Lorina.

"It's a way of putting things off," said the Sow, "in the hope that the problem will go away."

"But it won't go away!" cried Lorina.

"Of course not," said the Sow, picking up a piece of paper and hurriedly writing on it. "And that's why we must act at once. I want you to take this letter to Professor Tusker at the University. I'm appointing him Head of the Commission. Talk to him. He'll soon sort things out."

With the letter in her hand, Lorina quickly left the Sow's office and ran past the sty. The smell followed her for quite a long way, and so did the voice of the Sow, who was now singing a different song:

"Progress, progress, scientific progress,
Marching ever onwards to our place in historee.
We must take our chance
And steadily enhance
Our technical advance
For the sake of little…"

But Lorina didn't hear the last word, because she had finally gone out of earshot.

Chapter Eleven

THE PROFESSOR

Professor Tusker was sitting in his study, the walls of which were covered with books and pictures. When Lorina looked a little closer, she found that none of the books had titles, and the pictures were all blank frames. This seemed a little strange.

"Ah!" said the professor. "You must learn that the greatest art leaves everything to the imagination."

It still seemed strange, but Lorina had more important things on her mind than titleless books and pictureless pictures.

The professor read the letter from the Sow and grunted. He was very old, and although he was a sort of pig, he looked quite different from the others that Lorina had seen. He had a very dark face and coat, and two curved teeth grew on either side of his mouth. He was, in fact, an old bore.

"Well now," he said, "let's see… green people… dying… smoke, fumes, starvation, nuisance, time, blah… Commission of Inquiry… Right. And what do you want me to do?"

"Stop the furnaces," said Lorina.

"What do you mean by 'stop'?" asked the professor.

"Stop," said Lorina. "So that they won't kill any more green people."

"Do you mean put them out, dampen them down, intercept the smoke, block the chimney, close the doors, open the windows, give people masks, tell them not to breathe—"

"We must put the furnaces out," said Lorina. "That's the only way to stop the smoke."

"Who exactly do you mean by 'we'?" asked the bore.

"Well," said Lorina, "whoever puts furnaces out."

"That's not 'we'," said the professor. "You and I don't put furnaces out, do we?"

"It doesn't matter *who* puts them out," said Lorina, "so long as they *are* put out!"

"It doesn't matter to whom?" asked the bore.

"It doesn't matter to me," said Lorina.

"But it will certainly matter to whoever puts them out," said the bore, "so you can't say it doesn't matter."

Lorina was beginning to find this conversation rather annoying. It seemed to her that the professor was talking about all the wrong things.

"It doesn't matter whether it matters or not!" she snapped.

"Maybe it doesn't matter to *you* whether it matters or not," said the bore, "but that doesn't mean it doesn't matter to somebody else."

"I just want the furnaces to be put out!" cried Lorina.

"But furnaces can't just *be* put out," said the bore. "Somebody has to do the out-putting."

"Then the superviper can do it," said Lorina.

There was a moment's silence, during which Lorina had a feeling that at last she'd solved the problem. After all, the superviper was the one who gave the orders in the furnace building. Not even the professor could deny that.

"You're right," said the professor, very slowly. "Yes, you're right. The superviper can put them out. But will he? And if he won't, why should he?"

"The Sow can order him to."

"She *can*. But will she? And indeed, can she? Who says that she can? Is there a law that says she can?"

"I think you pigs can do anything if you really want to," said Lorina, "because you're in charge."

"Now that," said the professor, "is one of the silliest statements I've heard in years. 'We can do anything if we really want to.' I really want to live for ever, be young again, possess every book, picture and truffle in the world and play hoofball for the asses. Do you think I can, eh?"

"Well, no," said Lorina, "but that's not what I—"

"'We're the ones in charge.' In charge of what? Am I in charge of the sun, the moon, the weather, time, space, the Assenal hoofball team? Am I?"

"No," said Lorina, "but that's—"

"There you are then. You're talking nonsense."

"You're in charge of things in the Castle," said Lorina. "You can get things done in the Castle. So please, please help me to get the furnaces put out."

"How can I help you?"

"The Sow said you would head a Com… something of Inquiry."

"And that's just what I'm doing," said the bore. "I'm inquiring into everything you say, and so far everything you've said is nonsense. So come back when you can say something that means something."

Lorina gave up. In the Castle it didn't matter whether she knew more or less than those she was arguing with. She could never win.

As she left the professor's study, a piglet came skipping along the corridor, carrying a titleless book under its trotter.

"Hello, there!" it cried. "Have you just had a lesson with the professor?"

"Yes," said Lorina.

"What did he teach you?" asked the piglet.

"Nothing," said Lorina.

"What do you mean by nothing?" asked the piglet with a giggle.

Lorina didn't reply. She'd had enough arguments for one day.

Chapter Twelve

THE PIGGIDENT

At the entrance to the University was yet another statue of the Beloved Leader. As always, he was smiling, and Lorina recalled the song that had been sung at the hoofball match. Perhaps the Piggident *was* fine and the sweetest of swine. After all, a Beloved Leader must be loved for something, and it might be his kind heart. As leader he would surely be able to help the green people, for he could give orders for the furnaces to be shut down and for food to be sent out. Lorina wondered why she hadn't thought of going to him before.

The Piggident, she discovered, lived in the Royal Wing on the western side of the Castle. It had a beautiful entrance door, draped in purple cloth and with rich gold designs all round the frame; and on the door itself was an unusual pattern which looked like this:

I
me
myself
memememe
mememememe
myselfmyself
memememememememe
mememememememememe
myselfmyselfmyself
memememememememememememe
memememememememememememememe
myselfmyselfmyselfmyself
memememememememememememememememe
memememememememememememememememememe
myselfmyselfmyselfmyselfmyself
memememememememememememememememememememe
memememememememememememememememememememememe
myselfmyselfmyselfmyselfmyselfmyself
memememememememememememememememememememememememe
memememememememememememememememememememememememememe
myselfmyselfmyselfmyselfmyselfmyselfmyself
memememememememememememememememememememememememememememe
memememememememememememememememememememememememememememememe
myselfmyselfmyselfmyselfmyselfmyselfmyselfmyself
memememememememememememememememememememememememememememememememe
memememememememememememememememememememememememememememememememememe
myselfmyselfmyselfmyselfmyselfmyselfmyselfmyselfmyself

In front of the door, marching in four different directions at the same time, was a long thin creature with lots of legs and with a peaked cap over its eyes. It was a sentripede.

"Halt! Who goes there?" it called.

"Lorina," said Lorina.

"Hello, Lorina," said the sentripede. "I'm Pete. I'm... um... new to the job actually. You've no idea what I'm supposed to do next, have you?"

"I expect you have to ask me for the password," said Lorina.

"Ah!" said Pete. "Right, what's the password?"

"I don't know," said Lorina.

"Nor do I," said Pete.

"In that case, you'd better let me pass," said Lorina.

"Yes, all right, then," said Pete, and so Lorina walked through the door with the strange pattern, and found herself in the Royal Apartments.

The rooms were sumptuous. There were paintings on the walls and ceilings, linen and silver on the tables, cushions on the chairs, ornaments of gold and porcelain, glittering glass, foot-sinking carpets, thick velvet curtains... Lorina had never seen such opulence. At the far end of the biggest room, there was a throne of gold and precious stones, and sitting in this, wearing a purple robe and a jewel-encrusted crown, was the Piggident.

Feeling a little nervous, Lorina approached the throne. The Piggident was smiling.

"Hello," said Lorina.

The Piggident continued to smile.

"I… I've come about the green people," said Lorina. "They're starving, you see, and the smoke from the furnaces is choking them."

The Piggident said nothing. He just smiled.

"Are you all right?" asked Lorina.

Then she realized that he was not looking at her. In one trotter he was holding a round object of silver which had a long handle, and he was looking into this and smiling at what he saw. As she went closer, she saw that it was a mirror.

"Excuse me," said Lorina. And then a little louder: "Excuse me!"

He still didn't hear.

"Excuse me!" shouted Lorina at the top of her voice.

Without taking his eyes off the reflection in the mirror, the Piggident suddenly let out a loud sigh. It was the first sound, and indeed the first movement he had made. Lorina waited, and slowly the smiling jaws came together. He was going to say something. Still gazing into the glass, he finally murmured in a tone of the utmost wonderment a single word:

"Me."

Then there was a long silence.

"Can you hear me?" asked Lorina. "Can you see me? Do you know I'm here?"

It was useless. She even tugged at his purple robe, but he felt, heard and saw nothing. The Beloved Leader was in love with himself, and oblivious to the world.

Chapter Thirteen

THE ARREST

Lorina was tired and miserable – and hungry. She had had nothing to eat all day, and although she had made up her mind not to rest until she had helped the green people, it now seemed to her that she might help them better if she helped herself first. And so she left the Royal Apartments, and the lovesick Beloved Leader, and went to Mr Hogg's kitchen.

She was lucky. Mr Hogg was still there at the table, of course – for he was far too heavy to move – but he was fast asleep, and snoring like a furnace.

"So you've cookome back," said the cookoo.

"Yes," said Lorina, "and I'm hungry."

"Of cookourse you are," said the cookoo. "Have some cookorn flakes."

Lorina sat at the opposite end of the table from the rumbling pink monster, and the cookoo gave her a bowl of cookorn flakes. After that, she had some cookottage pie with cookauliflower, cookourgettes and cookucumber, followed by cookoconut cookake and cookustard, and finally a cookup of hot cookocoa.

"Ah, that's better!" said Lorina. "Now then, do you think you could give me a big bag of food to take to the green people?"

"Sh!" said the cookoo, shaking his head vigorously. "Cookeep your voice down!"

"Why?" asked Lorina.

"Becookause walls have ears," said the cookoo.

Lorina looked round, and found to her surprise that the cookoo was right: there were ears growing out of the walls.

"What are they for?" she asked.

"Secookurity," whispered the cookoo.

Lorina didn't see how ears could make the walls more secure, but the cookoo explained that the pigs liked to listen in on other animals' conversations, and that made the pigs feel more secure.

"But it's rude to listen in on other people's conversations," said Lorina.

"Sh!" said the cookoo again.

"If they hear what they're not supposed to hear," said Lorina, "then it serves them right."

The cookoo was afraid that it might serve him and Lorina wrong, and so he quickly gave her a big bag of food and hurried her out of the kitchen.

With food inside her, and food in the bag, Lorina felt a lot happier as she headed towards the Castle gate. Now she would be able to give something to the green people, and then she would come back and get things organized. Perhaps the cookoo would send them a bag of food every day.

As Lorina came near to the gate, the doormouse scurried out of his little office.

"Where d'yer think you're goin'?" he asked.

"Out," said Lorina.

"Wot's in the bag?" he asked.

"Food," said Lorina.

"Thought so," said the doormouse. "That ain't allowed."

"What isn't allowed?" asked Lorina.

"The hexportin' of Castle food," said the doormouse. "*You* c'n go out, but the food can't."

"Why not?" asked Lorina.

"Rules o' the Castle. I'm afraid I shall 'ave ter constipate this 'ere bag."

"Don't be silly," said Lorina. "Now open the gate and let me out."

As Lorina was much bigger than the doormouse, she did not expect to have much difficulty in getting out, but the doormouse stood resolutely in her way.

"Give us the bag!" he said.

"No," said Lorina.

"Then by the powers undervested in me," said the doormouse, "I 'ereby place you under arrest."

"You can't arrest me," said Lorina. "I'm bigger than you."

"The law," said the doormouse rather grandly, "is bigger 'n both of us. Yer under arrest."

"No, I'm not," said Lorina.

"Then you soon will be," said the doormouse, and gave a loud whistle.

Into the archway bounded two large black dogs.

"What's the trouble?" growled the first dog.

"She's the trouble," said the doormouse. "She refused to 'and over the bag, an' now she refuses ter be arrested."

"Right," snarled the second dog. "Hand over the bag."

Lorina usually got on well with dogs. She would say "Hello, boy" and pat a dog on the head, and then it would be her friend for life. But these dogs were not looking for a pat on the head or for lifelong friendship. They were looking for Lorina's bag. She quickly handed it over.

"And now you're under arrest," growled the first dog.

"We'll take 'er ter the dungeon," said the doormouse.

"With the greatest of pleasure," snarled the second dog.

The doormouse went to his office door and called out:

"Just goin' ter the dungeon, Mrs D. Look after the gate till I gets back, will yer?"

Then he returned to Lorina and the dogs, and he seemed to do a little skip as he walked.

"Great day, this is," he said. "Fancy me catchin' a criminal."

On the way he sang a little song:

"Put 'em in jail,
Put 'em in jail.
Only place ter put
Yer common criminail.

Lock 'em in the dungeon,
Let 'em sweat it out,
Then they'll see wot crime an'
Punishment's about.

Leave 'em in the darkness,
Shut the iron door.
Soon they'll start a-wishin'
That they 'adn't broke the law."

At the prison they were met by a fat bird with a bunch of keys, a bald head and a double chin. His brown-coated body seemed too heavy for his legs, and although there was not a horse in sight, he was wearing a pair of spurs. He was a turnkey.

"Brought you a criminal," said the doormouse. "Caught 'er smugglin' food an' resistin' arrest."

"Smugglugglugging food, eh?" said the turnkey. "Followollowollow me."

And so it was that Lorina found herself walking down a flight of stone steps that led into deepening darkness. The turnkey went wobblobblobbling ahead, and the doormouse and the two black dogs stayed behind her, to make sure that she didn't run away. At the bottom of the steps, the turnkey turned a key in an iron door, which Lorina could scarcely even see in the gloom. Then the dogs pushed her in, and the turnkey closed the door with a loud clang.

Chapter Fourteen

THE KING
OF THE CASTLE

Lorina sat on the stone floor, waiting for her eyes to get used to the darkness. She could hear rushing sounds accompanied by high-pitched twitterings, and she was aware of movements in the air all around her, but she still hadn't made out what they were when she was startled by a voice:

"No need to bow," it said.

Lorina looked around.

"I'm over here," said the voice. "In the corner."

"There are four corners," said Lorina.

"I'm in *this* corner," said the voice.

By now Lorina could make out the walls of the dungeon, and she could also see tiny shapes flying through the air. In one corner, a dim figure moved.

"Who are you?" she asked.

"I'm the King of the Castle," he said. "And who are you?"

"I'm Lorina," said Lorina.

"Pleased to meet you, Lorina," said the voice.

"What are these things flying through the air?" asked Lorina.

"They're the jailbirds," said the voice. "They're quite harmless."

Lorina could see him quite clearly now. He was small and dark (probably green, but it was difficult to tell in the gloom), and had long hair and a long beard. His clothes were ragged and scarcely even covered his thin body.

"You're probably thinking I don't look much like a king," he said.

"Well, yes, I was thinking that," said Lorina.

"I don't feel much like a king either," he said. "And I'm not actually king any more. I *was* king, but then the pigs took over, and they put me in here."

"Why did the pigs put you in here?" asked Lorina.

"I suppose they didn't like me," said the King.

"I don't like the pigs," said Lorina. "They're greedy and mean and selfish."

"That's power for you," said the King. "And why have they put *you* in here?"

Lorina told him her story. He was particularly interested in the green people, and when she mentioned Qasim he gave a visible start. She stopped for a moment, thinking that he wanted to ask her some questions, but he settled again and told her to go on.

"Are you green?" she asked.

"Yes," he said. "Now please go on."

She finished her story, and then there was a long silence. He seemed to be working something out in his head. Then at last he spoke again:

"There's been a lot of suffering," he said.

"It's the pigs' fault," said Lorina. "They refuse to feed the people in the north, and they're killing the people in the furnaces."

"In my day," said the King, "people didn't work in the furnaces, or in the fields. That was animal work."

"Do you know Qasim?" asked Lorina, remembering his reaction.

"Yes," he said, and there was something in his tone of voice that Lorina found disturbing.

"Are you enemies?" she asked.

"I don't want to talk about Qasim," he said. "I want you to tell me about the dogs…"

But there was no time for them to talk about the dogs, because suddenly the jailbirds started twittering very excitedly and fluttering their wings in a headlong rush towards the dungeon door. A moment later, it swung open, and in came the turnkey.

"Time for a nibblibblibble!" he called. "Come and get it!" The jailbirds gathered round him on the floor as he put down a large dish.

"Eat it all up!" he said. "Nothing for you two, though – unless you find birdseed enjoyableoyableoyable."

He went out again, locking the door behind him, but in the meantime, Lorina had had an idea.

"Listen," she said. "I think I know how we can escape!"

"Escape?" said the King. "That's impossible. These walls are six feet thick."

"Not through the walls," said Lorina. "Through the door. Next time the turnkey comes with the birdseed, we'll hide behind the door. As he's putting the dish down, we'll rush out and lock the door on him. Then we'll be free, and he won't be able to raise the alarm till long after we've got away."

"Now why didn't I think of that?" said the King. "I've been sitting here all this time, and it never occurred to me."

Lorina suddenly felt very tired. She had had a busy day, and now her legs wanted to stretch out, her eyes wanted to close and her brain wanted to stop thinking. The King promised to wake her up as soon as the turnkey came back, and so she lay down on the hard floor, cradling her head in her arm, and went to sleep. And as she slept, she dreamt that the jailbirds were flying in a circle round her head, and they were singing:

"Everything comes, everything goes.
What will become of us, nobody knows.
Summer is autumn, winter is spring,
The feather's a pen, the pen is a wing.
When the sun shines, the apples are sweet.
When the wind blows, they fall at your feet.
Roses are budding while the tree grows.
Swiftly, then, swiftly bottle the rose.

Ocean to clouds, clouds into rain,
Falling to ocean, rising again.
Everything comes, everything goes.
What will become of us, nobody knows."

She was woken by a gentle shaking, and the jailbirds were indeed singing, but the song was a loud twittering which Lorina could not understand.

"The turnkey's coming!" whispered the King.

Lorina jumped to her feet, and she and the King hid behind the door of the dungeon.

Chapter Fifteen

THE TRIAL

As soon as the door opened, Lorina knew that this was not the moment for escape. The turnkey was not alone. He had brought the two black dogs with him.

"Come alongalongalong, Lorina!" he called. "Time for your trial!"

"We can't escape now!" Lorina whispered to the King.

"No!" he whispered back. "Another time! Good luck!"

Lorina stepped out from behind the door.

"There you are!" said the turnkey. "Followollowollow me!"

He led the way up the flight of stone steps, and the black dogs snapped at Lorina's heels. At the top they were met by a brown bird with spots on its chest. It was whistling a merry tune when they arrived.

"This way, Lorina!" it whistled.

While the turnkey went back to his office, the brown bird (who was the court thrusher) and the two dogs walked along a passage which led to another flight of steps. There was light at the top of these, and Lorina suddenly found herself in a sort of box that overlooked a large room full of spectators. As soon as she appeared, there was a loud buzz of excitement.

"Is this another hoofball match?" asked Lorina.

"Of course it isn't!" whistled the thrusher.

"Si-i-ilence in cou-ou-ourt!" warbled a little bird that was sitting below Lorina's box. "Everybody ri-i-ise for His Porkship."

There was a loud rustling and scraping as all the animals stood, and then there was complete silence as the little bird (who was lark of the court) sang:

"Detur soli judice Gloria
Herewith thereby heretoforia
Omne ignotum pro magnifico
Inasmuchas quid pro quifico."

"What does that mean?" Lorina asked the thrusher.

"They're special legal expressions," whistled the thrusher.

"But what do they mean?" repeated Lorina.

"Sh!"

Through a door to the right of Lorina's box stepped a very, very old pig, who was wrapped in a black gown and had a curly white wig perched on top of his head. Slowly and ridiculously he doddered to his bench – which was even higher than Lorina's box – and lowered himself onto it. Then everybody else except Lorina, the two dogs and the thrusher sat down as well.

His Porkship the judge looked across at a box on the far side of the room, and there Lorina saw twelve small black snakes sitting upright in two rows of six.

"Mambas of the jury," said the judge in an old, cracked voice, "how do you find the prisoner?"

"Guilty!" came a chorus of twelve hissing voices.

"Wait a minute!" said Lorina. "You can't find me guilty before the trial."

"I can find you guilty whenever I like," said the judge. "Because I'm the judge."

"Then what's the point of putting me on trial?" asked Lorina.

"I don't know," said the judge, and leant down towards the lark of the court. "What's the point of putting her on trial?"

"*Ignorantia legis te excusat*," said the lark.

"Exactly!" said the judge. "Where's the Counsel for the Prosecution?"

"Here, Your Porkship," said a fierce-looking bird with piercing eyes and a hooked beak. He too wore a black gown and had a wig on his head. He was a legal eagle.

"And Counsel for the Defence?" asked the judge.

"She ha-a-a-sn't got one!" warbled the lark.

"Well, that proves she's guilty," said the judge. "Call the first witness."

"Bring in the bureaurat!" demanded the legal eagle.

The bureaurat took his place in the witness box.

"She didn't know the length of her left leg," he announced, "or how many hairs she has on the top of her head."

"Shocking!" said the judge. "She'll get ten years for that."

"Do you deny the charge?" asked the eagle.

"What charge?" asked Lorina. "I'll bet you don't know the length of *your* left leg."

"Of course I do," said the eagle. "It's the same as the length of my right leg."

Everyone in the court applauded.

"Well, I'll bet you don't know how many hairs you've got on your head," said Lorina.

"Yes, I do," said the eagle, removing his wig. "None at all."

He was a bald eagle.

"Brilliant!" said the judge, and everyone in the court cheered.

The next witness should have been Mr Hogg, but he had been unable to leave the kitchen table, and so the farmadillo took the stand. He said that Lorina had tried to stop him burning food.

"In other words," said the eagle, "she tried to stop you burning food."

"Yes," said the farmadillo.

"Does that mean she tried to stop him burning food?" asked the judge.

"It does, Your Porkship," said the eagle.

"Why is that a crime?" asked Lorina.

"Why is that a crime?" the judge asked the lark of the court.

"*Conflagrante delicto*," said the lark.

"Exactly!" said the judge.

Then it was the turn of the piggy banker, who said that Lorina had tried to make him give money away. A lot of the spectators gasped and booed, and the lark of the court had to call three times for silence.

"Give money away?" echoed the judge. "That's a capital offence!"

Next the eagle called for the PandA, but apparently he was asleep, and so it was the superviper who provided the next shock.

"Shshshe wantsss to exssstinguish the furnacccesss," he hissed, and once again there were gasps all round the court. His evidence was confirmed by the Sow, and then by the professor.

The final witness was the doormouse, who described in great detail how Lorina had tried to smuggle food out of the Castle, and had then resisted arrest.

"One crime after another!" cried the eagle. "And every crime proves that she is a criminal! That concludes the case for the prosecution."

"And very well argued too," said the judge. "Prisoner, what have you got to say for yourself?"

"I haven't done anything wrong!" said Lorina.

"Perjury as well," said the judge. "A dreadful case. I shall deliver my summary when we've had a break. I simply must do a diddle."

He stood up, and everybody in the court had to stand as well until he had finished hobbling out through his door. Then there was a general hubbub as all the spectators discussed the case.

"Excuse me!" said Lorina, leaning over to talk to the lark of the court. "Will I be allowed to defend myself?"

"N-o-o-o," warbled the lark. "You lost the ri-i-i-ght to defend yourself when you committed the cri-i-imes."

"Then when are people allowed to defend themselves?" asked Lorina.

"Only when they're inno-o-ocent," replied the lark. "Everybody ri-i-ise for His Porkship!"

Everybody rose again, and His Porkship creaked through the door and onto his bench.

"Ah," he said, "that's better. Now then, let me summarize this most difficult and complex case. The crime must fit the punishment, and so it is clear that a rolling stone gathers no rosebuds in the merry month of May, and a stitch in time is like a needle in an hourglass. Look before you pee. Any pot in a storm. The pun is mightier than the swearword. The leopard does not change its nappies, and the hand that rocks the cradle smacks the bottom. In for a penny, you've got it cheap, the early bird catches a chill, there's always room at the bottom, and please throw us a few of those pearls. United we stand, divided we stand twice. If at first you don't succeed, give up. A friend in need is no friend of mine. And never speak ill of a judge. I must therefore ask you, mambas of the jury, what is your verdict on this guilty prisoner?"

"Guilty!" hissed twelve snaky voices.

"Are you unanimous?" asked the judge.

"Yes!" squeaked a little whiskered animal who was looking after three even littler whiskered animals.

"Oops, sorry!" (She was a nanny mouse who had misunderstood the question.)

"Yesss!" hissed the jury.

The judge beckoned to a little grey bird with a dark crown, and it flew up from its seat in the front row and perched on top of the judge's curly wig. It was a blackcap.

"I hereby sentence the prisoner," said the judge, "to be taken down to the dungeon and there to remain until I've had a good rest. She shall then be taken from thence and have her head chopped off. Twice."

"You can't chop my head off twice," said Lorina.

"Two beheadings are better than one," said the judge. "Take her away."

Thereupon the court thrusher nodded to the two black dogs, who nipped Lorina's legs until she found herself running down the flight of steps that led from the court towards the dungeon.

Chapter Sixteen

THE KEY

The court thrusher was annoyed to see that the turnkey was not waiting at the end of the passage. He should have been there to take Lorina down the second flight of steps, and as the thrusher had no intention of going all that dark way down to the dungeon, he ordered the dogs to take Lorina there. The dogs seemed strangely reluctant to do so.

"You go first," said the first dog to the second, "and I'll follow."

"I've got a better idea," said the second dog. "*You* go first, and *I'll* follow."

"Why don't you both go first, and *I'll* follow," suggested Lorina.

In the end, though, it was Lorina who went first, and the two dogs followed.

When they were about halfway down the steps, they suddenly heard a loud banging. The dogs immediately bounded up the steps again and stood trembling at the top.

"Who's there?" called Lorina.

"W-w-we are," said the dogs.

"I didn't mean you," said Lorina. "Who's that knocking?"

"It's a ghost," said the first dog.

Lorina went down a few steps further.

"Who is it?" she called.

The banging became even louder, and a muffled voice shouted: "Helpelpelp!"

"It's the turnkey," said Lorina. "He must have got locked in the dungeon."

Sure enough the dungeon door was locked, and sure enough the turnkey was behind it.

"Helpelpelp! Helpelpelp! The King's escaped!"

Lorina smiled to herself, and she smiled again when her foot trod on a key. She bent down, picked it up, and slipped it into her pocket.

"Let me out! It's horriblorriblorrible in here!"

By now the two dogs had very cautiously come down the steps, and stood looking from Lorina to the door and back to Lorina again. Lorina knocked on the door.

"Where's the key?" she asked.

"I don't know!" screamed the turnkey.

"Where's the key?" Lorina asked the dogs, but they didn't know either. And Lorina certainly wasn't going to tell them, because she wanted to give the King as much time as possible to get away.

"You'd better go and get a spare key, then," Lorina said to the dogs.

"I'll go," said the first dog. "You stay here and guard her."

"No, I'll go," said the second dog, "and you can stay here and guard her."

"Maybe I should go," said Lorina, "and you can stay here and guard each other."

The dogs thought this was a good idea, but the turnkey (who took his job very seriously) shouted that Lorina was the prisoner, so she shouldn't go anywhere, and one of the dogs must go.

"I've got a key here," said Lorina, "and I'll put it in one of my hands. Whichever of you chooses the correct hand can go and get the spare key."

The dogs agreed, and the second dog correctly chose the hand with the key in it.

"Best of three!" cried the first dog, but Lorina said you had to make that kind of rule *before* the game, and so the second dog ran up the steps to fetch the spare key. Meanwhile, Lorina sat with her back against the dungeon door, and the first dog sat down with his back against Lorina. She noticed that he was trembling.

"Why are you trembling?" she asked.

"I'm af-f-fraid of the d-d-dark," he said.

"Then close your eyes," said Lorina, "and pretend it's light."

The dog closed his eyes, but then opened them again because he said it was even darker when they were closed.

The second dog reappeared at the top of the steps.

"Where *is* the spare key?" he called.

Lorina asked the turnkey, and the turnkey said it was in his coat pockypockypocket. The second dog went away again.

"What's your name?" Lorina asked the first dog.

"H-H-Hero," said the dog.

"That's a nice name," said Lorina.

"I g-g-got it because I'm so b-b-brave," said the dog.

The second dog – whose name was Nero – reappeared at the top of the steps.

"Where *is* the coat?" he called.

Lorina asked the turnkey, who said he was wearing it. Nero pointed out that he couldn't very well get the key from the turnkey's coat pocket if the coat was locked inside the dungeon. The turnkey screamed that in that case he would never get out of the dungeon, but Lorina – who was now beginning to feel rather sorry for him – suggested that maybe he could take the key out of his coat pocket and open the dungeon door himself.

There was a rattle of key in keyhole, the dungeon door swung open, and out came the turnkey – to the accompaniment of much merry twittering from the jailbirds.

"What a calamalamalamity!" he cried. "The humil-imilimiliation! Locked in my own dungeon!"

By now a good hour had gone by, and Lorina reckoned the King should have made his way out of the Castle. In any case, the turnkey seemed in no hurry to raise the alarm. He proceeded to tell Lorina, Hero and Nero how the King had jumped on him when he went to feed the jail-birds, had pushed him down onto the dungeon floor, and had then run off, locking the door behind him.

"Lucky I had my spare key with me," he said, "or I'd have been in real troublubblubble."

He invited them all to his office for a drink to celebrate his miraculous escape, and so they climbed the steps again. It was while they were drinking a glass of good strong tea that Lorina realized why he was in no hurry to raise the alarm.

"I've got a problobloblem," he said. "If anyone finds out the King's escaped, I could well end up jobloblobless and headleadleadless, so let's pretend he's still in there."

Lorina was quite willing to keep quiet about the King's escape. She was also, to the surprise of the turnkey and the dogs, quite willing to go back into the dungeon. Of course, they didn't know she had the key. As it turned out, however, there was no time for her to get in, let alone get out, for just as she was about to go down the steps again, the court thrusher appeared at the door to the turnkey's office.

"His Porkship the judge has had his rest," whistled the thrusher. "It's now time for the execution."

Chapter Seventeen

THE EXECUTION

The execution was to be held in the courtyard where the hoofball match had been played. It was the only yard big enough to hold all the spectators. As the court thrusher and the two dogs brought Lorina in, there was a loud cheer, which continued as she was led to the middle of the arena. There in the centre was a raised platform, on which sat His Porkship the judge and the lark of the court. In front of them was a box with a notice that read: "PLEASE PUT HEAD ON TOP AND KEEP STILL".

The thrusher and the dogs took Lorina up some steps and onto the platform.

"The prisoner, Your Porkship," whistled the thrusher.

"Ah yes," said the judge. "Nice to see you again, my dear."

"You're not really going to chop off my head, are you?" asked Lorina.

"Of course not," said the judge. "That's the oxecutioner's job."

The Piggident now made his usual smiling, waving entrance onto his balcony, accompanied by several other pigs, and the lark of the court led the crowd in singing "We lo-o-ove our glo-o-orious Lea-ea-eader". The glorious and Beloved Leader smiled and waved again, and then sat down to enjoy watching himself watching the show.

"Bring in the oxecutioner!" shrilled the lark of the court, and another loud cheer echoed round the yard as the oxecutioner came in. He was a bull-like creature, carrying a huge axe, and he had to be guided towards the platform because he was wearing a mask.

"Why does the ox with the axe have a mask?" Lorina asked the thrusher.

"The ox with the axe has a mask," whistled the thrusher, "because the axe cracks the necks on the box."

"I know the axe cracks the necks on the box," said Lorina, "but why does he need a mask for the task?"

"I don't know," said the thrusher.

By now the ox was standing on the platform.

"Excuse me," said Lorina. "But why does an ox with an axe need a mask for the task of cracking the necks on the box?"

"Because I can't stand the sight of blood," replied the ox.

The judge now ordered Lorina to kneel down and put her head on the box.

"Wait a moment," said Lorina. "If he can't see anything, how does he know where to swing the axe?"

"That's a good question," said the judge, and repeated it to the lark of the court.

"By the law of *Fortuna favet fatuis*," replied the lark.

"This is no time for legal nonsense," said the judge. "I'm sitting in the line of fire here."

The lark explained that the ox would be relying on luck, whereupon the judge said he'd prefer the ox to rely on eyesight, and ordered him to remove his mask.

"But I'll faint!" complained the ox.

"Then shut your eyes!" said the judge.

Lorina pointed out that if the ox shut his eyes, he'd be just as blind as if he wore his mask. The judge asked her what she would suggest, and so she suggested cancelling the execution.

By now the spectators were slow-handclapping and singing: "Why are we waiting?"

"The spectators wouldn't like that," said the judge.

"I would," said Lorina.

The lark of the court suggested that the ox should keep his eyes open until the very last moment, and then shut them. Everybody except Lorina agreed that this was a good idea, and so the judge again ordered her to kneel down.

"No," said Lorina.

"You can't say no to a judge," said the judge.

"Yes I can," said Lorina. "No."

After a few more kneel-downs and a few more noes, the judge ordered the dogs to give Lorina a nip and a bite.

"Sorry about this," said Hero.

"Orders are orders," said Nero.

And a heroic nip in the left leg, followed by a neroic bite in the right leg, finally brought Lorina to her knees.

"Now I'll just say a few words," said the judge, and creakily rose to his feet. The crowd fell silent.

"Death," said the judge, "is final."

Everybody applauded, and so he sat down again.

"Tell the ox to aim at the box," he said to the thrusher. "I don't want any whacks with his axe."

The thrusher passed on the order, the ox raised his axe, took careful aim and...

"*Stop!*" cried a loud and very authoritative voice.

The ox left his axe up in the air, Lorina lifted her head from the box, and all eyes turned in the direction of the voice. It belonged to a green man who had a long beard and was wearing a crown on his head.

"It's the King!" cried a chorus of voices. "Boo! Boo!"

The King strode through the crowd and climbed onto the platform.

"Boo! Boo! Down with the King!" shouted the crowd.

"*Dogs!*" cried the King, and suddenly into the courtyard came the same pack of dogs that had controlled the crowd at the hoofball match. In no time they were nipping and biting the legs and feet of the spectators.

"Please can we go and do some nipping and biting too?" asked Hero and Nero.

"Yes, if you like," said the King, and the two bounded off the platform and into the crowd.

Very soon the spectators were shouting: "Hurray! Hurray! Up with the King!"

Lorina was now on her feet, the ox had lowered his axe and His Porkship the judge was asking the lark of the court to explain what was happening.

"Listen carefully, everybody!" cried the King, and the crowd fell silent. "I am your king, and from now on things will be exactly as they used to be before I stopped being king. Go to your places of work. You'll find my green people in command now. Do as they tell you, and then life can get back to normal."

Some of the crowd started to boo again, but the dogs did a bit of nipping and biting, and the boos turned to cheers.

"How did you get the dogs to obey you?" asked Lorina.

"Dogs will obey anyone they think is in authority," said the King. "Besides, I promised them the best bones in the Castle."

"Excuse me," said the judge, "but is the execution going ahead or isn't it?"

"Yes and no," said the King, and snapped his fingers. Two dogs leapt onto the platform. "Help His Porkship to join his fellow pigs," ordered the King, and the judge found himself wobble-limp-hobbling off the platform.

"Where's he going?" asked Lorina.

"Don't worry about him," said the King. "His judgement days are over. Come along – you and I have something to celebrate."

"Um… what about me?" asked the ox with the axe.

"Oh, go and do some ploughing," said the King.

As Lorina left the courtyard with the King, she noticed the judge and all the other pigs being herded through a door in one corner. Again she asked where they were going.

"Breakfast," said the King.

Chapter Eighteen

HOW TO BE A KING

As they walked through the Castle, Lorina was surprised by how quickly all the animals had disappeared. Apart from dogs shepherding the occasional stray creature from one area to another, the only living beings were green people, who would immediately stop and bow to the King. Lorina looked out eagerly for Tanga and Birim and Qasim, but there was no sign of them, and when she asked the King about them, he simply murmured: "All in good time."

They eventually came to the Royal Wing. Beside the richly draped entrance with its strangely patterned door stood Pete the sentripede.

"Halt! Who goes there?" he cried.

"The King, you fool," said the King.

"Oh, sorry, Your Majesty," said Pete. "I'm still a bit new to the job."

Inside the Royal Apartments were a lot of green men in bright uniforms.

"Has the place been thoroughly cleaned?" asked the King.

"Yes, Your Majesty," replied one of the green men.

"Good," said the King and, turning to Lorina, he explained: "The pigs were here."

"I know," said Lorina. "I saw the Piggident here."

"The Piggident!" laughed the King. "Our Beloved Leader! I'm having all those ridiculous pictures and statues taken down as soon as my men have finished cleaning up."

They sat down on one of the plump, plush sofas, and the King ordered tea.

"Now then," he said, "you're bursting to know what's been happening, eh?"

"Yes," said Lorina. "Are Tanga and Birim all right? And Qasim? And have you stopped the smoke, and—"

"Slowly! Slowly!" said the King. "One thing at a time. Let me tell you the story from when we were separated."

He described to Lorina how the turnkey had come to feed the jailbirds, and he'd put her escape plan into operation. Then, while her trial had been going on, he had gone to the dog kennels and persuaded the dogs to join him. After that, he and the dogs had brought all the green people out of the southern fields and the factories. They had silenced any animals that had got in their way. Lorina wondered what he meant by "silenced", but it would have been rude to interrupt the King.

The one tricky moment had come between the trial and the execution, but the dogs had pretended that everything was normal. Most of the animals that had been in the court had gone straight to the hoofball yard anyway, and would not have noticed anything. The green people had taken over all the positions of command, and so now he was King again and in complete control of the Castle.

"It was simple," he said. "The vital thing, of course, was to get the dogs on my side. But none of this would have been possible without you, Lorina, and I'll see that you're properly rewarded."

"But what about Tanga and Birim and Qasim?" asked Lorina.

"Ah!" said the King. "Well, frankly, I wouldn't worry about them if I were you."

"But I *am* worried about them!" said Lorina.

"They're outsiders," said the King. "And so they don't really matter. It's insiders that count."

"They *do* matter!" said Lorina. "You've got to help them!"

"Got to?" said the King. "Got to? A king hasn't got to' do anything. A king makes other people do things. That's why he's king."

Lorina felt her heart sinking.

"And the smoke?" she said. "Aren't you going to stop the smoke?"

"Of course not," said the King. "Without the furnaces, there'd be no power to drive the engines."

"But the smoke is killing Tanga's mother, and all the other people outside!" cried Lorina. "Can't they at least come inside?"

"What for?" asked the King.

"They're your own people!" said Lorina.

"They may look like me," said the King, "but they're outsiders. They're not 'my people'. Besides, what would be the point of bringing them in? We'd only have to feed and clothe and house them. There are enough of us here already. No, no, Lorina, you mean well, but you have to learn how things work in the Castle. It's all very well having a kind heart, but kind hearts don't rule castles. Here, have a chocolate biscuit."

Lorina did not want a chocolate biscuit. Lorina wanted to feed the green people outside and to stop the smoke. She also wanted to ask some questions.

"What did you mean by 'silencing'?" she asked.

"Silencing?" repeated the King.

"You said you silenced some animals," said Lorina.

"We did to them," said the King, "what the judge was going to do to you."

"You killed them?" asked Lorina.

"It's a good way of silencing," said the King.

"And what did you mean when you said the pigs were going to breakfast?" asked Lorina.

"Out of the dirtiest pig," said the King, "comes the crunchiest bacon."

"You are a bad king!" said Lorina. "You're greedy and mean and selfish and cruel!"

"Did I ever say I wasn't?" said the King. "But if you go on insulting me, I shall become an even worse king, so watch your tongue."

"I won't!" said Lorina. "Now I understand just why the animals locked you up. You're cruel to them and you're cruel to your own people, and I wish I'd never helped you to leave the dungeon!"

"If I hadn't left the dungeon," said the King, "you'd have been left without a head."

"Two lefts don't make a right," said Lorina. "You're more of a pig than the pigs, and you shouldn't be king!"

"That's it," said the King, "that's enough, that's more than enough, that's as much as I'm prepared to listen to. Steward!"

In came one of the uniformed green men.

"Take this creature to the dungeon, and warn the turnkey not to go inside when he feeds the jailbirds. Maybe, Lorina, when you've sat there for a few years, you might learn to respect a king."

And so it was that Lorina found herself yet again on the way to the dark, damp dungeon.

Chapter Nineteen

IN AGAIN, OUT AGAIN

"You again?" said the turnkey. "What's the troublub-blubble this time?"

Lorina told him.

"So there's been a revolevolevolution, has there? Well, it won't make much difference. Pigs one day, green peopleopleople the next, it's all the same."

And so saying, he locked Lorina in the dark again, and the jailbirds flew round her head, making sympathetic twittering sounds.

Of course, what the King, the turnkey and the jailbirds didn't know was that nestling in Lorina's pocket was the key to the dungeon door. A plan was already forming in her mind, but she would have to stay in the dungeon for a few hours yet, and try to guess when it was night-time.

Lorina lay down to rest, and once again fell asleep on the hard stone floor and dreamt that the jailbirds sang to her:

"Everything comes, everything goes.
What will become of us, nobody knows.
Children skip, stick in hand,
Waves to rocks, rocks to sand.
Tresses fair shade to grey,
Stars of night fade to day.
Blushing grape upon the vine,
Falling, falling into wine.
Present lives are only tales,
Wrinkled faces only veils.
Everything comes, everything goes.
What will become of us, nobody knows."

When she awoke, once again she heard the jailbirds twittering, but she could not understand them.

"Why do you sing such sad songs?" she asked, but then immediately wondered if the songs *were* sad. Perhaps they were only sad if you thought they were sad.

She judged that it was now time for her to escape. Quietly, she unlocked the dungeon door and crept out, locking it again behind her. There was no sign of the turnkey, but when she climbed the steps and went past his office, she saw him fast asleep in a corner, with his doublubblubble chin shaking up and down as he snored. It occurred to her that he was as much a prisoner as she had been.

When she left the prison building, she found that night had indeed fallen, and the whole Castle was wrapped in silence and moonlight. One side of the courtyard was illuminated, and the other was in darkness, and there was no movement anywhere except for an occasional swirl of shadow as a cloud crossed the moon.

Lorina made her way to the dog kennels. Here, too, everything was quiet, but as she approached the first kennel, a doggy voice suddenly called out:

"Wotcher!"

"Um… hello," said Lorina.

"Wotcher name?" asked the voice.

"Lorina," said Lorina.

"Wotcher want?"

"To see Hero and Nero."

"Wotcher wanner see them for?"

"I've got something for them."

"Wotcher got for them?"

Only now did Lorina realize that the voice belonged to a wotcherdog.

"I've got a job for them," she said. "From the King."

"Pass," said the voice.

Lorina walked past, and in the bright moonlight began to peep into the kennels, looking for Hero and Nero. There were all kinds of dogs fast asleep in their little huts, and they were making all sorts of sounds: a sheepdog was baaing, a bulldog was bellowing, a husky was coughing, and a boxer was shouting, "Nine, ten, out!" There were some strange sights too: a pointer kept jerking his front leg, a lurcher rocked from side to side and a retriever was running round in circles.

At last, Lorina found her two friends, sleeping in neighbouring kennels. She woke Hero first, but the moment he saw her shadowy figure in the moonlight, he screamed, "Yoiks! It's a ghost!" and dived into the far corner of his kennel.

When Nero saw the figure against the moon, his eyes opened as wide as dog biscuits and his jaw hit the floor of the kennel with a clunk. The rest of him refused to move.

"It's me! Lorina!" said Lorina, and eventually the two dogs crept dog-sheepishly out of their kennels.

"Now listen," said Lorina, "we've got a very important job to do for the King."

Since the dogs didn't know that Lorina and the King had quarrelled, this sounded interesting. They had visions of royal headpats, medals and top prize in the Dog of the Year Show.

"This is what we have to do," said Lorina. "The King wants us to take some food to the green people in the north."

"I like taking food," said Nero.

"I prefer eating it," said Hero.

"That's not all," said Lorina. "There's a green man in the Royal Wing who's pretending to be king. The real King wants us to take him out of the Castle as well."

"Um… is he a *big* green man?" asked Hero.

"No," said Lorina. "He's about the same size as the King. It'll just need a few nips and bites."

"I'll do the nipping," said Hero.

"And I'll do the biting," said Nero.

And so the three of them quietly set out towards the Royal Wing.

"Wotcher doin'?" asked the voice from the first kennel.

"Important business," said Lorina.

"Then wotchyer step," said the voice.

On the way to the Royal Wing, they stopped at Mr Hogg's kitchen. In the moonlight that shone through the window, Lorina could see a large dark patch on the floor by the kitchen table, but of Mr Hogg himself there was no sign. The cookoo wasn't there either. Lorina quickly found a large bag and filled it with bread, fruit, cakes, vegetables and chocolate biscuits. She also noticed some piles of fresh ham and bacon, but decided not to touch them. Nearby lay a pair of scissors, and these she picked up and slipped into her pocket.

"Where do they keep the bones?" asked Hero.

"We haven't got time for bones," said Lorina.

"I always have time for bones," said Hero.

"Not now," said Lorina. "The King will be angry if we're late." It was time for the most dangerous part of their mission: capturing the man who was pretending to be king.

Chapter Twenty

THE KINGNAP

When they reached the moonlit entrance to the Royal Wing, they met their first obstacle.

"Halt! Who goes there?"

"You can see perfectly well who goes there," said Lorina. "I'm Lorina, and these are Hero and Nero."

"Just testing," said Pete the sentripede. "Hi, Hero. Hi, Nero."

"We want to see the King," said Lorina.

"Then you've come to the right place," said Pete. "Just say the password."

"The password," said Lorina.

"In you go," said Pete.

They left the bag of food for Pete to guard, and made their way to the royal apartment. The sound of kingly snoring led them to the royal bedroom, and Lorina quietly opened the door.

"Now remember," she whispered, "he'll pretend that he's the King, so take no notice of what he says, make a few growls and give him a good bite if he resists."

There was a nightlight burning in the bedroom, and Lorina could see the King lying on his back, mouth open and long beard waving in the breeze. She took the scissors out of her pocket, and with two big snips she cut off the beard. Then she leant over and gave the King a good shake. He stopped snoring, closed his mouth, opened his eyes, saw Lorina, opened his mouth and said, "What…?"

"Get up," said Lorina.

"What… what?" gasped the King.

"Quickly," said Lorina, "or the dogs will eat you."

Hero let out a grim growl and Nero uttered a snorty snarl, and the King quickly got out of bed. He was wearing red pyjamas, and he put his feet into a pair of red slippers with big white bobbles.

"You can't do this!" he said. "I'll have you all executed!"

"Good imitation!" said Hero.

"Very convincing!" said Nero.

"Get your dressing gown on," said Lorina, and the King put on his red dressing gown.

"I'll have your head!" he said to Lorina. "And I'll have your bones!" he said to the dogs.

"Scary, eh?" said Nero.

"Good job he's not the King," said Hero.

"He doesn't even look like the King, does he?" said Nero.

"Not without his beard he doesn't," said Hero.

A nip from Nero and a bite from Hero sent the King on his way through the corridor and out of the front door.

"Halt! Who goes there?" demanded Pete.

"You don't have to ask people coming *out*," said Lorina.

"No, I know," said Pete, "but it gives me something to do. Who's your friend?"

"I am the King," said the King, "and I order you to arrest this girl and these two dogs."

"He's a joker," said Hero.

"Pretending to be the King," said Nero.

"I *am* the King!" said the King.

"There he goes again," said Hero.

"The King's ordered us to throw him out," said Nero.

"I'm being kingnapped!" cried the King. "Arrest them!"

"He does sound like the King," said Pete.

"But everyone knows the King's got a long beard," said Lorina.

"That's true," said Pete.

"And who's ever seen a king in pyjamas and dressing gown?"

"That's true too."

"I was in bed, you idiot!" cried the King. "And she cut off my beard!"

"And that proves he's not the King," said Lorina.

"What does?" asked Pete.

"He called you an idiot," said Lorina. "Are you an idiot?"

"No," said Pete.

"Well, if he was the King," said Lorina, "he would know that, wouldn't he?"

"Yes, he would," said Pete. "Pass."

Lorina made the King carry the heavy bag of food, and they set out on their way towards the

Castle gate. There was no sign of the doormouse, and so Lorina rang the bell at the door of his lodge. She had to ring several times before eventually a little window above the door (it was a doormer window) was opened, and a tiny head poked out.

"'Oo is it?" asked the owner of the head.

Lorina explained that she was on an important mission for the King, and the gate must be unlocked immediately.

"'Old on a minute," said the voice.

There was another delay, and then the lodge door opened.

"You'll 'ave to ask me dad," said a tiny whiskered creature in pink pyjamas. "Come in."

Lorina bent low and entered the lodge. She followed the minidoormouse up some stairs into a large room with rows of beds on either side, all filled with minidoormice. It was the doormitory. And right at the far end, fast asleep in a double bed, lay Mr and Mrs Doormouse.

"Wait till I've got back into me own bed before yer wake 'im up," said the minidoormouse. "'E don't like

bein' woke up. An' we ain't s'posed ter get up 'cept in emergencies."

The doormouse was not at all pleased to be woken up. He said a few naughty words which brought giggles from one or two beds at the side of the room. But when he heard that Lorina was on the King's business, he grumpily stumped down the stairs, lifted his bunch of keys off a hook on the wall and went outside with her.

The King at once informed him that this was a kingnap.

"Yer lucky ter get *any* nap in my job," grumbled the doormouse.

He opened the gate, and Lorina and the dogs pushed the protesting King out. The doormouse never even noticed the bag of food.

"Good riddance!" he said, slamming the gate behind them. "An' don't come back till midday!"

Chapter Twenty-One

QASIM AND WASIM

By the time the party had descended the smoky hill, dawn was breaking, and as they drew near to the camp of the green outsiders, the sound of singing reached their ears:

"Thy body lies beneath the earth,
Thy holy soul departs.
Though thou art gone, we love thee still
And hold thee in our hearts.

Let us rejoice that thou wast here
To bring us warmth and light.
Now after weary toil of day
Rest peaceful through the night."

The singing ceased, and then Lorina heard a clear, deep voice saying the following:

"She is the rock on which all castles stand,
The root and blossom, source of life and love.
Between our coming hence and going thither
She is the nourisher that never fails,
Giver of light even to those in darkness,
For those in darkness have most need of light.
She is confessor, refuge and inspirer,
The shoulder of our leaning and our crying.
And in her passing passes that most holy
Of all the human virtues: selflessness."

There was a moment's silence, during which Lorina thought she heard a child's sob. Then the voice went on: "Even as we mourn our beloved sister, let us give thanks for her life and for the lives of those she leaves behind her."

A group of green people were standing round a grave, and among them Lorina could now see the tiny figures of Tanga and Birim. The deep, clear voice was that of Qasim, who led the people in a prayer of thanksgiving.

"She died!" murmured Lorina. "Tanga and Birim have lost their mother."

Lorina, the King and the two dogs stood to one side, and the King made no complaint but kept his head bowed, as if reading the earth.

When the burial was over, the circle of green people dispersed, but Qasim had seen the visitors, and came towards them. The King lowered his head still further.

"You came back," said Qasim to Lorina, and nodded when he saw the bag of food. "And who have you brought with you?"

He reached out, and gently lifted the chin of the King.

"It's you!" he said.

The King lowered his head again.

Qasim called one of the green men over and gave him the food to distribute. Then he called Tanga and Birim, and put his arms round them.

"We shall not forget your kindness," he said to Lorina. "Come with me now, all of you."

They followed him to his tent, where they sat in a semicircle. Qasim again enfolded Tanga and Birim in his arms, while Lorina had Hero and Nero on either side of her. The King sat a little apart.

"Do you know who this is?" Qasim asked Lorina, gesturing towards the King.

"Yes," said Lorina. "He's the King."

"No he's not," said Hero.

"He's *pretending* to be the King," said Nero.

"He is the King," said Qasim, "and he is not the King."

"I don't understand," said Lorina.

"His name is Wasim," said Qasim, "and he's my younger brother. He had me driven from the Castle so that he could make himself king, and I and my people have suffered ever since."

"I've suffered too," said Wasim. "I was locked in a dungeon."

"You deserved to be locked in the dungeon!" said Lorina. "You were a bad king."

"I wasn't a bad king," said Wasim. "I was very well loved."

"Who by?" asked Lorina.

"Me," said Wasim.

Lorina remembered the Piggident, who had also loved himself, and she wondered how such creatures managed to get into power.

"How did Wasim get you driven out of the Castle?" she asked Qasim.

"By secretly promising wealth to those who'd support him," said Qasim, "and by promising meat to the dogs."

Lorina looked at Hero and Nero, who were shuffling their paws and shifting their bottoms.

"Sorry," said Hero. "We were only puppies then."

"We won't do it again," said Nero.

"You *have* done it again," said Lorina.

"Have we?" asked Nero.

"He offered you bones, so that you'd let him be king."

Hero looked at Nero, and Nero looked at Hero, and they both looked at Wasim, who looked at the ground.

"That's right," said Hero, "and we haven't had them yet!"

"I'll let you have them as soon as you get me back to my throne in the Castle," said Wasim.

"You're not going back to the throne," said Lorina. "Because you're not the King."

"Exactly!" said Nero.

"You're only pretending," said Hero.

At this moment, Tanga gently detached herself from Qasim's protecting arm and walked across to Lorina.

"Will you be our mother now?" she asked.

Lorina embraced her.

"I can't," she said. "I'm only a little girl myself."

Birim detached himself from Qasim and walked across to Wasim.

"Will you look after us?" he asked.

"No, Birim, no!" cried Tanga. "He's a bad man! Leave him alone!"

She ran to Birim, seized his hand, and brought him across to Lorina.

"I don't think he's bad," said Birim, looking back. "I think he's just unhappy."

Wasim's eyes suddenly clouded, and he turned his head away.

"What's going to happen to us?" Tanga asked Lorina.

"It's obvious what has to be done," said Lorina. "You'll go back to the Castle, and you'll find a new home there with a nice family. Qasim will be King again and everyone will live happily ever after – everyone except Wasim, who can live unhappily ever after. The good people must win, and the bad people must lose – that's how all the best stories end."

Everyone apart from Wasim thought this was a good idea, and Qasim asked Lorina if she would go back to the Castle with them.

"I can't," said Lorina. "I've got to go to school tomorrow."

"Then will you come and visit us one day?" asked Qasim.

"Oh yes," said Lorina. "I'd like to do that."

Qasim stood up, and as he did so, the sun streamed through the entrance to the tent.

"Thank you for helping us," he said. "We'll never forget you."

Then he was gone, and a moment later Lorina heard him calling the people to prepare for their journey. The deep, clear voice rang through the stillness of the morning, and he said, "We are going home."

"Come on, Birim," said Tanga. "We must go too. Goodbye, Lorina."

Lorina kissed Tanga, but Birim was not yet ready to leave. He went again to Wasim, who was still sitting on the ground, looking miserable.

"You can come with me," said Birim, "if you want to."

He held out his hand. Wasim took it, rose to his feet and, without looking at Lorina, left the tent.

"We're… um… a bit confused," said Hero.

"Confused?" asked Lorina.

"The man we kingnapped," said Nero. "Is he the King or isn't he?"

"Or was he the King or wasn't he?" asked Hero.

"It's quite simple," said Lorina. "He was the King but he wasn't and now he isn't."

"Oh!" said Hero.

"Ah!" said Nero.

When Lorina and the dogs left the tent, the green people had already assembled for their journey to the Castle. There were more goodbyes, and then they all began to move slowly in the direction of Castle Hill, while Lorina walked towards the hill that would take her down into the forest.

When she reached the top, she turned, and through the smoke and the haze of the morning sun, she could just see the party of green people stretched in a line from halfway up the hill to the gate of the Castle. She waved, but they were too far away for her to see whether they were waving back.

Then she turned again, and began the descent towards the forest.

Chapter Twenty-Two

GOING HOME

"They didn't eat you, then?" said the black rabbit.

"Who?" asked Lorina.

"The outsiders, of course," said the black rabbit.

"Not at all," said Lorina. "The outsiders are lovely. You got things the wrong way round. It was the insiders who were horrible."

"Nonsense," said the black rabbit. "How could the insiders be horrible? They live inside the Castle. It's the outsiders – the green people – they're the horrible ones. Everybody knows that."

"I've seen them and you haven't," said Lorina.

"You've been hoodwinked," said the black rabbit.

"Anyway," said Lorina, "the green people are all inside the Castle now, and the King of the Castle is a green man, so there won't be any more outsiders. They're all going to be insiders."

"Don't you believe it," said the black rabbit. "Going inside isn't going to change them. Once an outsider, always an outsider. Once green, always green."

"The trees are green in summer," said Lorina, "but they change to brown in the autumn."

"Trees are trees," said the black rabbit. "Trees change, but people don't."

It was just as difficult to talk to the black rabbit on the way home as it had been on the way to the Castle. Lorina had been surprised to see him again, but he had been waiting for her as soon as she had reached the thicker part of the forest. She wondered how long he'd been waiting, but when she asked him, he pretended not to hear.

"Anyway, I've got some good news for you," she said, "about the forest."

"I don't believe in good news," said the black rabbit. "The only news you can believe in is bad news."

"Well, I think they'll stop cutting down the trees now," said Lorina. "They were burning the trees in their furnaces, but I'm sure they'll find another way to drive their engines."

"Oh yes?" said the black rabbit. "What's that, then? Burning rabbits?"

"You *are* a misery!" said Lorina.

He went with her all the way to the edge of the forest and to within sight of her home. She invited him in for a cup of carrot juice, but he said he must be getting back – and so she thanked him for helping her, and hoped that he would one day find something to make him happy.

"I *am* happy," he said.

"You don't sound it," said Lorina.

"You've made me happy," said the black rabbit.

"How?" asked Lorina.

"Because I'm always happy when I win an argument," he said. "And I always win arguments when I'm with you."

Away he went, and Lorina watched him disappear into the trees. She wondered if he would be there if she ever wanted to find the Castle again. Then she wondered if the Castle would be there.

When Lorina got home, her sister asked where she'd been.

"We've had people out looking for you," she said.

CHAPTER TWENTY-TWO

Lorina told Edith about the Castle and her strange adventures.

"I'll bet it was a dream," said Edith. "Adventures like that are always dreams."

Lorina shook her head.

"Maybe yours are," she said. "But mine wasn't."

"Well, you'd better get on with your homework," said Edith, "or you'll never have it ready for tomorrow."

Lorina went to her room, took out her exercise book and began to write: *I walked into the forest…* But then she stopped and crossed it out. Something wasn't quite right about that. She started again: *I met the black rabbit…* But then she stopped again, and crossed that out too. After a long pause, she started again: *Lorina walked into the forest and met the black rabbit…* This seemed a lot better, but she still felt uncomfortable.

"Maybe it shouldn't begin with Lorina at all," she said. And then she began again:

"You should know," said the black rabbit, "that there are two kinds of people at the Castle…"

And from that moment, she didn't stop until she had finished writing the whole story.

David Henry Wilson is a children's author and playwright, best known for his *Jeremy James* and *Superdog* series. His books have been translated into many languages including Spanish, German and French. He has also written numerous plays, including *People in Cages*, and frequently works as a translator from French and German.

Chris Riddell has illustrated and written of an extraordinary range of books and has won many awards, including the UNESCO Prize, the Kate Greenaway Medal (three times) and the Hay Festival Medal for Illustration. In 2015 he was appointed Children's Laureate.